I0626332

BITTER BLOOD

ZARA HOFFMAN

Bitter Blood.
Copyright © 2020 Zara Hoffman.
Bitter Blood/Zara Hoffman – 1st ed.
ISBN 978-0-9991986-4-3

Book Cover Design ©2017 White Rabbit Book Design

All rights reserved.

This is a work of fiction. Names, characters, and incidents are a product of the author's imagination. Locales and public names are sometimes used for atmospheric purposes. Any resemblance to actual people, living or dead, or to entities, events, or locales is completely coincidental.

No part of this book may be reproduced in any form or by any electronic or mechanical means, including information storage and retrieval systems, without written permission from the author, except for the use of brief quotations in a book review.

To Natalie:
Your friendship and expertise helped me launch this trilogy & I'm
forever grateful

TRIGGER WARNING

Please be aware that this book involves kidnapping and sexual
attraction between the prisoner and captor.

If this is triggering for you, please take care of your mental health
and skip this book.

And then I am going to rattle the stars.

SARAH J. MAAS

1

VERITY

VERITY PICKED up the note again and ran downstairs, the piece of paper gripped tight in her hand. "Hey, Dad?"

"Yes?" he called from the kitchen.

She rounded the banister. "Was someone here?" she asked, forcing her voice to stay level. The last thing she needed was her father to hear a tremor. If he knew she was scared, he would freak out. And one of them needed to keep a calm mindset if they were going to handle things effectively.

His posture stiffened and he shook his head. "Why?"

She handed him the note.

Verity watched him read it, his face passing from red to purple. She could see a vein in his forehead emerge as it pumped angrily. If her father weren't so fit and had to watch his blood pressure, she'd be concerned for his health. Though, given his recent head injury the night of her abduction, it was still probably a bad idea for him to be so stressed out.

She took the piece of paper back. "Calm down. We don't want you ending back in the hospital."

"*Calm down?*" He took a step forward. "You're telling me to *calm down* after everything that's happened in the past month?"

She winced and shrank back a step. She knew his anger wasn't actually directed at her, but she wished she could disappear and escape the evil eye he was currently aiming at her.

Poor choice of words on her part. On every count possible: to her dad, who was a General in charge of over 300 personnel and understandably was on edge regarding her safety. If she didn't watch her mouth, she'd probably be restricted to base before she could breathe another word. Which meant reminding him that it had only been twenty days instead of a full thirty or even thirty-one was an awful idea.

"There was an alien in this house! One who kidnapped you! And I had no idea." His next words were much softer. "I couldn't protect you."

If her father were a more touchy-feely person, she'd have given him a hug, or even touched his arm to comfort him, but he had never been like that.

The best thing to do was to distract him by getting back to business. "No alarms went off?"

Her father pulled out his phone and pulled up the security app. Together, they watched the recording of their entry way from that morning but nothing appeared. Then, at the last moment, she saw a blur of motion coming in the door and a second later, the same blur leaving and the door closing. It happened so fast, it was a wonder that the door hadn't splintered or snapped off its hinges.

"Did you see that?"

"See what?"

She pointed to the screen where the blur had barely registered. "Someone was there." It had to be Knox. Unless he'd sent Aerue as a messenger. It probably wasn't Trohm, who had been held under lock and key since they got back but she couldn't rule out the chance that he had broken free. Their chains on Earth were nothing compared to what they'd put on her but for him to get into her home before her when he had gone without a fight toward the opposite side of the base where the cells were made no sense. Whoever it was, he was wearing alien cloaking technology which made it impossible for her to tell which one had come in uninvited. Which meant one or both of them were on Earth. She swallowed the lump in her throat. That couldn't be good news.

Her father grunted. "I didn't see anything." He pulled the phone closer and squinted as he replayed the recording.

She knew it wasn't going to do much. His vision was already close to perfect, genes she had inherited. If she could see it and he couldn't, there had to be a special reason.

Was this another instance of her being able to do something others couldn't? Like when she could see the doors or read the speaker button on the ship?

"Well," she said, handing him back the device. "One of them got in and left."

Her father's face paled. "Are you sure they're gone?"

She nodded. That was the only thing she was sure about.

"What do we do?" she asked. It's not like getting a new alarm system would be helpful. They already lived on the most secure military base in the country and the aliens had proved twice over now that getting in—especially their home—was no challenge.

Her father walked into his office. She trailed after him and listened to his side of the conversation with whomever he called. "Get someone from cyber over here... Now."

"You should also ask Zeph to check it out," said Verity.

If anyone was going to figure it out, an ASE scientist was a better bet than one of her father's STF's. They were great at fighting, and some of them were even good at technology but it wasn't their primary domain, so why not recruit someone who did it day in and day out?

He gave her a sidelong glance but passed along her request. A few more moments passed before he hung up.

"He's been debriefed and is available to help. Go change. They should be here soon."

Verity looked down at herself, having completely forgot she was just in a towel. She ran upstairs, taking them two at a time, and quickly threw on a light sweater and shorts. It might be summer, but her father always ran hot and constantly had the air conditioner blasting. Which didn't help the fact that she always ran cold except while sleeping at night.

Wearing a sweater also had the bonus of rendering a bra unnecessary. She didn't like to wear them when she didn't have to. After three weeks of being constricted by clothes forced upon her and cuffs, she wasn't about to wear something uncomfortable when she had the choice not to.

She slipped a hair tie onto her wrist before heading back downstairs.

Exactly five minutes later, the doorbell rang.

She wasn't exactly sure where they had put up Zeph but given it probably wasn't in any of the dorms or the base hotel, the arrival time was something. Knowing the urgency, however, maybe he had just grabbed a bus to get there faster.

She went to answer it, but her father practically bodychecked her out of the foyer. He moved in front of her and checked the security screen to verify it was who they were expecting.

Verity bit back her comment that the aliens wouldn't ring the doorbell or wait for them to welcome them inside. And him blocking them with his body wasn't enough of a barrier based on Eiz'm's demonstrated strength.

Looking over her father's shoulder, she could see a small image of a man she didn't recognize wearing a patrol cap waiting outside with his hands behind his back. Zeph stood beside him in a polo shirt and cargo pants. Clearly, someone had either loaned him some clothes or he'd gone shopping at the base exchange.

Clearly satisfied, her dad finally admitted them.

The Cyber Dog—a nickname given to people in the weapons division—removed his cap, tucking it under his arm. He nodded in greeting toward her then followed her father to the security room.

Zeph waved and smiled at her before trailing behind the other men. She brought up the rear and watched them all hover over the array of screens connected to the cameras mounted all over their home, both inside and outside.

She had always assumed he had gone overboard with the number of security devices when they already lived in one of the most secure places on earth. She'd been wrong, but now she could see that he'd taken it a step forward and multiplied his efforts in fortifying their home against future breaches.

Her father pulled up the footage in question onto the center monitor before moving out of the way for the cyber guy to sit down.

Verity stayed near the threshold and watched as the tech typed away at her father's keyboard.

Her damp hair was starting to seep through her top, chilling the back of her neck and the space between her should blades. As much as she wanted to go dry her hair, there was no way she was going to miss any of the action here.

He dragged the cursor over the section of the screen in question and zoomed in but it did nothing to clarify the image.

Different application windows popped up and closed at a rapid pace but nothing helped.

Her father didn't say anything but his frustration loomed over them, like a growing vacuum, sucking the air out of the room.

Finally, the Cyber Dog rose and said, "I'm sorry, sir. That's the best I can do."

Her father nodded, dismissing the young man.

She moved out of the way for him to leave, not taking her eyes off the screens.

Zeph took the vacated seat and started typing away.

From her point of view, it looked like he was repeating the exact same actions as his predecessor but all of a sudden, the enlarged image re-rendered without any blurs of motion, clearly showing a dark figure standing in their home.

It was much better than what they had before but it didn't offer any new information that she hadn't already seen with her naked eye.

"I can't clarify the image any more than this, General Landau," Zeph explained, "but someone was definitely here."

"Thank you, Mr. Powell," her father said.

She glanced back at her new acquaintance. His last name didn't fit him. It was too stuffy for someone who's nickname name was as cool as *Zeph*. But she supposed "Joseph" didn't fit someone her age, either. Maybe his parents were just old fashioned. Or were living under a rock. She couldn't think of another explanation for how they could be so out-of-touch with modern names.

"Of course, sir. I wish I could do better but the system isn't capable of slowing down the footage any more. No current security system is."

"But is it possible?"

"There are cameras capable of intense super slow-motion," Zeph explained, "but to have them running constantly on the off chance of recording something like this would take an incredible amount of energy and digital memory that it's not a sustainable system worth—"

"My daughter's safety is absolutely worth it."

His voice brooked no argument but he had to see how unreasonable he was being.

"Dad—"

He shot a glare at her over his shoulder.

She shut her mouth, swallowing the rest of her protest but refused to break eye contact. He might be pissed at her, but as his daughter, she wasn't going to let him steamroll everyone. Just because his protective father instincts were going into overdrive didn't give him the right to be an ass.

"Of course, sir. I didn't mean to imply otherwise," Zeph said in a surprisingly level voice. "But the cameras are also prohibitively expensive."

"If I got a set, could you hook them into the security system?"

"Dad!" There was no way they could afford it, and even though the government could probably foot the cost, it was still a huge ask and wasn't a good long-term investment.

"I didn't ask your opinion, Verity," her father responded. He checked his watch. "We have a spare closet on the first floor that could be converted."

Verity knew which one he was talking about. It used to serve as a guest closet when they actually *had* guests. Her mother would invite her father's coworkers from the base over for lunch or dinner every so often. Since she died, however, it had mostly just been her and her father in the house. The closet now only held their coats for easier access near the front door.

I'm going to call a meeting. You're staying here until I get back. I'll send a guard over to keep watch. Mr. Powell, I'll walk you out."

"Wait." The word was out of her mouth before she could stop it.

Both men turned toward her, waiting for her to continue.

"Can Zeph stay?"

Her father's gaze jumped between the two of them. She could practically see the wheels turning in his mind.

"We barely got introduced before we commandeered one of their ships to come back home," she continued. Hopefully that would dispel any mistaken conclusions he was drawing.

"I'll have Captain Tenner sent over."

"Thank you."

"Stay downstairs."

Verity blushed at the implication but didn't argue. There was no reason to aggravate him, and it would only encourage the wrong idea.

"Later, you'll both have to be debriefed about your time..." he trailed off, seemingly at a loss for words to describe their ordeal. He pursed his lips before turning toward the door.

They watched her father leave, before they moved or spoke again.

She led Zeph into the kitchen. "Do you want something to drink?"

"What do you have?"

She opened the refrigerator and scanned the contents. There was orange juice and her father's beer. He clearly hadn't refilled her stock of energy drinks while she was gone. She probably should've checked before she offered.

"We have water or orange juice. Sorry. I thought there would be more options."

He shrugged. "No worries. I'll just have water."

She grabbed two glasses from the cabinet and filled them with filtered water. "Ice?" she asked.

He shook his head.

She handed him the glass and they sat down at the kitchen table, silently drinking in silence until her guest spoke up.

"Your dad is..."

"Yeah," she added. "I know he can be a bit scary, but he means well."

"I was just going to say he's intense, but I guess it makes sense with everything that happened."

"So, I never really saw you around on the ship." Granted, her time and focus had been completely filled with one of four different men at any given time. "What was your experience like?"

"Well, besides eating and being questioned a lot, nothing much."

"They didn't beat you?"

He shook his head. "But they hurt you, right?"

She nodded. "I'm better now, though."

Zeph's eyes quickly gave her a once over. "I can see that."

She couldn't help the blush that rose to her cheeks. "What did you tell them?" she asked, getting back to the topic at hand.

"Nothing. I just gave them false information."

Why hadn't she thought of that? Or Ben, for that matter? "And they didn't figure that out?"

"I pretended just lied in response to their questions. There was no reason for them to beat the answers out of me because they thought I was giving it to them freely—well, out of fear. Besides, I don't think they really cared about us, anyway. I kept hearing rumblings about you and Captain Tenner."

Why hadn't she thought of that tactic? It would've been better probably giving herself brain damage by getting herself knocked out by Eiz'm. She leaned forward, curious. "What kind of rumblings?" Apparently, the aliens liked to gossip as much as humans.

"They thought the king was spending a lot of time with you."

She snorted. "Well, that's not untrue." But she had no idea that the aliens gossiped like humans did. Though, given how petty Eiz'm acted towards her to spite Knox, she supposed she shouldn't have been surprised. There were a lot of similarities between their species she never would have expected before she met them.

There was a knock at the door before she heard the key turn in the lock.

Verity stood up, ready to fight if necessary. She heard Zeph also stand.

Ben walked in, and she relaxed.

He took off his ball cap, even though her father wasn't around, and headed toward them. It bore the STF motto *et pugna ad astra*, which roughly translated to "I fight the stars." It was a shame the squadron was a highly-classified government secret because it was such a cool motto that she would have loved to wear on a sweater while in dance class.

He took a seat at the table and she poured him a cup of water.

Today, he was wearing a simple t-shirt and shorts, clearly off duty for the day aside from being assigned as her babysitter. She would've felt bad, but honestly, she was glad to spend time with him without a ton of guards scrutinizing their every move.

He nodded at Zeph in greeting.

Verity rolled her eyes. Guys.

"Why is your hair wet?" Ben asked.

"I showered. How else would it get this way?" She grabbed a dish towel and started wringing out her hair again. Normally, she didn't care too much about air-drying her hair when she didn't have anywhere to be but she had a suspicion she was coming down with a cold. And her mother had always warned that having wet hair could make you sick, though she still couldn't figure out if there was any truth to that or if it was an old wives' tale.

"Have you been debriefed yet?" she asked.

He nodded but didn't offer any other details. Not that it mattered. She knew what he probably said and she'd likely be answering the exact same questions once it was her turn.

Once she felt the fabric completely soak through, she hung it up on the stove's handle and started French-braiding her hair. After her mom had died, she learned how to do it herself from watching videos and could now do it without a second thought. She hadn't needed a mirror in years.

She noticed Zeph watching her movements with thinly veiled interest but he didn't say anything.

Ben was watching her, too, over the rim of his glass as he took a long drink.

Was braiding hair really that impressive? She almost asked

them but decided against it. Instead, she asked, "How have you been?"

Ben shrugged, and she wanted to shake him until he gave an actual answer. He must have seen something in her expression because he finally said, "Glad to be home."

"Same," she agreed. "Where are you staying, Zeph?"

She tied off her braid and waited while he finished his drink.

"Some civilian housing outside the base that ASE maintains for when we visit you guys."

And he still got here the same time as the Cyber Dog? Wow.

"But I was being debriefed when your father summoned me."

She must be really transparent if he could read the question in her eyes. For Ben to do it made sense after years of friendship, but she'd just met Zeph. Maybe his scientist brain made him more attuned to small details.

Verity stood up and refilled all their glasses. "Did my dad tell you how long his meeting will be?"

Ben shook his head.

Well, what were they supposed to do in the meantime? "Um... do you guys want to watch a movie?"

"No rom-coms," Ben said.

"I should pick one just to punish you for that, but I actually don't have any. I have the classics." And by that, she meant her father had collected remastered versions of his favorite movie franchises. She opened the TV console revealing the options.

"Your dad likes the *Alien* trilogy?" Zeph asked.

"Not that," she said. "I need a break from all things extra-terrestrial for a while."

"You do realize you live at Groom Lake, right?"

"You don't have to remind me. Pick anything else."

Ben walked up and grabbed a fantasy film and popped it into the player before either her or Zeph could say another word.

She motioned them toward the couch and headed back into the kitchen to heat up some microwavable popcorn.

She'd never hung out with Ben like this and she could easily see herself becoming friends with Zeph. It wasn't the same as her and Ben and Tristan—Trohm—but this new normal could work out very nicely if today was any indication.

When she returned with the bowl, she took up the empty spot between them and settled in to watch the movie.

2

KNOX

KNOX DOUBLE-TAPPED THE CONTROL, turning off the pod and stepped out of the pilot's seat. On the outside, he dragged his fingers across the surface in fractal pattern and waited for the ship to disassemble.

It was already invisible to the human eye and though he had parked the vehicle far away from any residential area and inside a cave, it was still a popular tourist attraction and he didn't want anyone accidentally bumping into his only means of transportation. This way, the humans could walk over the pieces and never be the wiser.

If a human could actually see it, it would look as if it were disintegrating, permanently self-destructing. Its appearance was deceptive. While the ship really was breaking down, it wasn't irreparable damage for Eochronians, only to enemy species who would be unable to reassemble the pieces to use their technology against them. Not even the intelligent Lielneh had managed to reverse engineer the system, though he bet it wasn't due to lack of effort on their part.

He'd be able to find it again regardless, thanks to the tracker concealed in his uniform. And even if some of the pieces got scattered around the cave or carried away by the wind, they would be summoned back to the initial location. In a true emergency, he could even change the formation point to his current position as long as he had his armor.

No one was around right now but he kept the camouflaging capability activated and his helmet on as he climbed out of the cave. Verity's ability to fight his soldiers made it obvious she could see through their cloaking technology. The average human wouldn't be able to distinguish him from the environment as he moved toward his target.

Had the entire Air Force not been searching for him, he would have parked closer to the base but as that was not the situation, he had opted to set his destination for the neighboring state of California. Now, he just had to get across the border unnoticed.

Once Knox was a safe distance from it and had almost reached the road in front of him, he turned off the camouflaging and stored his helmet into his collar. Then he modulated the output to appear like he was wearing human clothes. He didn't want to raise any suspicion. He continued walking until he reached the road.

He saw a young woman driving from 500 yards away. He walked into the road and waited for her to stop. Then he slowly approached the passenger side.

When the driver didn't roll down the window, he knocked on it to grab her attention, then held up his hands to show he wasn't holding a weapon.

Finally, the glass pane lowered two inches. The young woman's curly red hair stuck to her forehead and her pale skin was flushed from the summer heat. Her bright green eyes were wide with fear.

"I'm sorry to bother you," he said as gently as possible, "but I'm stranded. Is there any chance you could drive me somewhere?"

"Where are you going?"

"Nevada. Don't worry, I'm not expecting you to take me the whole way there. I'm just trying to get to the border."

"Actually, I'm heading in the opposite direction." Her response was prompt but not too quick and her voice was level, but he knew she was lying. Her heart rate had kicked up a notch and her glance to the left was a dead giveaway.

"I promise I'm not a psycho."

"That's exactly what a psycho would say." He watched her reach for the key in the ignition to restart the car.

Before she could, he brought his hand up to the back of his neck, as if wiping away sweat even though his skin was dry and free of perspiration. He spoke again. "If you could just drive me to the border, that's all I ask."

He'd never done it with Verity, but royal Eochronians were blessed with persuasive abilities due to certain genes that allowed them to amplify their pheromones and modulate their voice to better appeal to people. As far as he knew, it only worked on non-Eochronians so he hadn't bothered to try using it on the captured subjects aboard his ship.

This time, the woman's eyes glazed over slightly. "Sure," she replied, unlocking the door with the tap of a button.

Before she could change her mind, he climbed in and told her where he wanted to go.

"Of course," she said. "It should take only a little over an hour. Are you in a rush?"

"An hour should be fine, but the sooner I get there, the better. I'm supposed to meet a friend there tonight and I accidentally got dropped off in the wrong state by my bus."

She glanced at him. "How did that happen?"

He shrugged. "I must have made a mistake with the directions."

"That's unfortunate."

"It is." He smiled at her and added, "Thank you so much."

The woman blushed and turned her focus forward again.

"Do you mind if I sleep?"

She wasn't being particular talkative but in case her curiosity eventually loosened her tongue, if she thought he was asleep, he could avoid any questions he didn't have answers to.

A nice perk of his persuasive abilities was he didn't have to be awake for the effect to work. Otherwise, he'd have to stay awake to make sure she didn't come to her senses and realize that she had been persuaded to act against her instincts.

His unwitting driver nodded, not taking her eyes off the road as she signaled a lane change.

He leaned back in the seat and closed his eyes, enjoying the sun on his face. Earth was much closer than where they'd been stationed near Jupiter. The last time he was this close to a star was back on Khavraid, though Qurqrik was much stronger than Earth's sun.

Their ship was very effective at collecting starlight and focusing it but it was a system that took time and still paled in comparison to experiencing a star's heat without any barriers aside from a planet's natural atmosphere.

This hour-long ride would keep him set for at least a human week without needing sleep. As he soaked in the rays, Knox still hadn't decided whether he was telling the truth or not but he wasn't against the idea of genuinely sleeping. He hadn't gotten any rest in a while. And the sleep he had gotten hadn't been restful since he met Verity. And he doubted it would be for the foreseeable future until his plan came to fruition and he was able to get the troublesome human female out of his system once and for all.

The heat loosened his muscles, and he felt himself quickly slipping closer to sleep until he let his mind go blank.

He woke to his driver politely clearing her throat.

"Is here good?" she asked.

Even without his enhanced Eochronian sight, he was able to see a sign welcoming him to the state of Nevada.

"Yes. This is perfect. Thank you so much for your help."

"My pleasure," she said. "I hope you have a good visit with your friend."

He watched her drive away. Once he was sure she wouldn't be able to see him, he donned his helmet again and turned his camouflage back on, becoming invisible again as he crossed the border.

AS KNOX APPROACHED the row of houses, he had to give his mole credit for finding a beautiful and unassuming home.

He walked up to the front door and unlocked it with the secret biometric hidden in the seemingly mundane peephole. The human Aeronautical Space Exploration organization may own the building but he had been assured that they had no idea about the Eochronian modifications his mole had made. If he'd been added into a human facial recognition or iris scanner system, there was the possibility that it would have eventually been discovered. By using their own system, it was undetectable by everyone on the planet aside from his agents.

He heard the door unlock and opened it, revealing a small but cozy living space. It was sparsely decorated compared to what had been described of the interior of Verity's home. He assumed other humans were more like her than his man but his agent was smart enough to not stand out too much by having only a few pieces on the walls. A collection of black and white and color images of space. None of them showed anything close to their home planet, not that he expected them to. Human technology hadn't ventured far enough from Earth to capture even the slightest glimpse of Eochronian and

A black and white image of what the humans had nicknamed the *pillars of creation* hung over an angular, gray couch. The furniture was thin, simple, and boxy, all following the same color scheme without too many design flourishes. The style was called minimalist, if he was remembering correctly.

Stripes of light lay across the space, so Knox closed the shades before proceeding further into the house. The two bedrooms were both small and roughly the same size, but he opted for the smaller one. He may be royalty but wasn't about to kick his agent out of his bed.

Knox opened the closet doors and found a few pants and button-down shirts. They weren't exactly his style and with the size difference between him and his agent, he wouldn't be able to use these clothes without people noticing. He'd have to go buy some eventually but that would have to wait for now.

Sitting on the side of the bed closer to the window, he opened a communication link to Aerue by saying his name forward then backward. Even with the semi-transparent shades closed, the sun's heat still warmed the room.

Knox smiled. He was definitely going to enjoy his time on Earth.

A life-size and life-like holographic imprint of Aerue appeared before him projected by nanotechnology not yet achieved by humans though similar systems had appeared in some of their more recent films according to his sources. His guard and friend's broad shape dwarfed the simple room. His head appeared to almost touch the ceiling. Aside from Aerue's inability to physically affect Knox's current surroundings, one could mistakenly think he was really there. "What are you so happy about?"

"The sun is great."

"Don't rub it in."

"You can use my personal solar chamber while I'm gone, you know."

His friend nodded but they both knew he never would.

Knox was a stickler for respecting roles, seniority, and

authority when it came to giving orders and properly addressing people—especially with rebellious people like Eiz'm—but Aerue insisted on adhering to decorum, even on the minutia of life. Permission from his king to do something that apparently transgressed those boundaries wasn't enough for Aerue to actually act.

"Did you run into any problems?"

Knox shook his head and gave a quick run-through of what he had to do to get close to the air base undetected.

"And you're sure this woman won't report having driven a strange man across a state border?"

"I'm sure."

"If only a certain human female were so accommodating to you."

Knox rolled his eyes. Half the fun of her was her challenging him. He wouldn't trade her spitfire nature for one of obedience even if he were given the choice.

"What are you intending to do down there?" Aerue asked. "Trohm might have been compromised but we already have other ones who are still protected and giving regular updates."

"I want to experience it for myself. We're eventually going to be living among them and second-hand information is only good up until a point."

His friend gave him a look that made it clear how unconvinced he was. "True, but you're rushing this. You could have waited until the serum was distributed and changes were starting to happen. It's too soon for new numbers to be infiltrating the planet."

"Aerue, I know what I'm doing."

"I'm telling you my honest and professional opinion, Your Majesty. Please consider what I'm saying."

His title only came out during their discussions when Aerue likely wanted to rage at him but never would.

"I am," Knox insisted. "But I'm being careful. They're not going to notice one more person."

"You can't guarantee that, Your Majesty. Ever since her abduction and return, they have been on high alert for us. If something were to happen to you, your plan will be for naught."

"It won't come to that, but even if it did, you're my second-in-command. They would listen to you if you led them along the same path."

"I'm not so sure. Eiz'm has been sowing seeds of discontent. His words are gaining more traction with your absence. You need to come back and rule from your rightful place on the throne."

"In good time," he replied. "I'm trusting you to handle the situation until I get back. I will keep you updated on my plans."

Aerue nodded, though Knox could tell he was dissatisfied with their conversation. "Be careful."

Knox said his friend's name backward then forward to sever their connection.

Walking into the remaining room on the first floor, he found a desk with papers bearing the ASE logo and a small metal cube that could easily be mistaken for a paperweight. He drew the proper glyph on each side, taking care to draw the circles and lines with precision or he'd have to start again. Once he was done, he waited for the small hum that indicated the successful unlocking of its contents. The box unfolded until it lay flat on the desk, revealing numerous images of members from the human airbase and space headquarters. The buildings were all imposing but he was only amused by as the extensive armory documented.

He chuckled. He'd be able to easily avoid their target-tracking missiles. They couldn't track what couldn't be seen at all. It wasn't about what they could see with the naked eye. None of their satellites or infrared surveillance systems would be able to detect him or his ship, and heat signatures were out of the question, leaving the missiles nothing to lock on to.

He turned his attention back to the people. There were some older men in suits, men and women wearing white coats with the

ASE logo embroidered on a chest pocket often filled with writing instruments, and soldiers wearing camouflage uniforms that would only effectively hide them in a forested area.

Why the humans called it camouflage when in reality it drew so much attention except for certain circumstances baffled him.

Then he reached the images of Verity, and couldn't help but smile. She had been a beautiful child. He had to guess her to be seven in the earliest one. There was a fair number of them given she was the only female candidate and had been tagged as such early on in her life by one of his deepest, undercover moles.

Once she got older, there were more photos of her with her Captain, and eventually her with Trohm. In some, she was being carried by her Captain on his back, other times, she merely walked beside him under his arm. She only came up to the men's hip at first before reaching her current height. And though that was still shorter than both the human and his mole, her presence more than made up for it. The three of them had been good friends and he could only imagine how she must have felt at discovering his betrayal. Pissed beyond belief, to say the least.

Similar to how she'd probably react to him once they eventually came face to face again.

Until then, however, he would keep his distance and settle into the human world. Which meant he needed to take a trip.

3

VERITY

VERITY TRAILED after her father through the base buildings. She would normally easily keep pace with him, but her legs felt like jelly for some reason, and she didn't want to randomly collapse in front of whoever may pass by. So, she walked at a slower pace where she felt solid enough on her feet that she could hide her anxiety.

Her father was already stressed enough about her capture and return and she didn't need him having another fatherly freak-out.

Her father showed his badge, though at this point it was a formality. They'd been on this base since she was three years old. Everyone knew who he was except for new hires. But there hadn't been any in over two years. Turnover was incredibly low at their base due to the intense vetting process and secrecy involved.

Everyone had signed non-disclosure agreements but if someone wanted to upload information to a conspiracy website, there wasn't much the government could do. A ton of people would see the post before it could be taken down and the person responsible dealt with. This normally meant they had assets seized and were threatened with being put on a terrorist list.

She hadn't heard of too many instances but one was already one too many in this case.

Her father put his keys and phone through the conveyor belt. He normally never brought keys with him unless he was leaving the base but he'd actually locked the front door as they left because being the base clearly had insufficient security. He stepped through the metal detector.

Then, it was her turn. She showed her badge, dropped her phone into the small bin and watched it go through the scanner until the guard motioned her to walk through the metal detector. She did and though no alarms went off, the guard stopped her and double-checked her with the wand detector.

She watched her father nod as he stared at the guard searching her before he turned his attention to stare intently at the monitor. What was he expecting to happen?

When the examination came up empty, she was allowed to pass.

Her father opened the elevator bank with an iris scan. She followed him inside and waited while he selected the third floor. They turned right into his wing and she saw a man and a woman, both wearing suits, waiting in the sitting area. His was black and hers was a dark navy.

Her father raised his hand and motioned for them to follow. All four of them walked into the conference room. No one said a word as her father pressed his hand to the scanner and then entered the nine-digit code to activate the Sensitive Compartmented Information Facility system, effectively turning the room into a a large black box full of secrets. Nothing would get out. There would be no information leaks.

The man held out his hand toward her father. "Hello. I'm Special Agent Kaur."

When he didn't offer his hand to her, her father cleared his throat, prompting the man to show her the same courtesy. She fought the urge to roll her eyes. She already didn't like this guy.

The woman shook her father's hand and hers in quick succession without hesitation. "I'm Dr. Jessica Hudson. Nice to meet you both, though I wish it were under better circumstances."

Doctor? She already had one of those. The same one ever since they relocated to Groom Lake. And her father had said she had an appointment with her after this debriefing, so why was there a second doctor here?

"Shall we get started?" Special Agent Kaur cut in, taking a seat at the table.

God, she wanted to punch him. He wasn't the most senior person in the room and it was clear this was her father's meeting, which meant it was his right—not this interloper's—to initiate it.

"Verity, are you ready?" her father asked.

She nodded. Best to get it over with. Like ripping off a bandage. The sooner they were done, the sooner she could get away from this clown of a Special Agent.

Only after her father sat down at the head of the table did she and Dr. Hudson seat themselves.

Verity sat on her father's right side while Mr. Douche was directly across from her on her father's left side. The good doctor sat on the agent's other side. Both of the visitors removed notepads and pens from their suit jackets' inner pocket, poised to write down her answers.

"You were abducted three weeks ago. The first week of August, correct?"

She nodded. There wasn't an audio recording as any listening devices would have been confiscated upon entering the building so it didn't matter if she gave nonverbal answers.

"Tell me what happened that night."

"I was sleeping but a sound woke me up. Then my dad told me there was an intruder in the house and I heard him fighting them downstairs." She left out the code name for the drill. The

CIA didn't need to know everything about the STF operations, and if her father wanted him to know, he could always chime in.

For some reason, she also decided to hide the fact that she had been able to see the spaceship before it landed, albeit only briefly.

"My dad," her eyes flitted to him to see he was watching her intently. She took a silent, shallow breath. She didn't want anyone here knowing her voice almost cracked. "He lost the fight, and they came upstairs to my room."

"How many were there?" the agent asked.

"Two."

She watched him write it down before continuing.

"I fought them off as best I could but then a third one came in and I couldn't escape all of them. They brought me onto their ship and then we left Earth."

She saw the woman make a quick notation of something and wished that she could read her writing upside down. She'd gotten out of practice since she started college but she used to do it all the time while bored in high school and elementary school.

Special Agent Kaur leaned forward. "What happened next?"

"I was put into a line with the other people who were abducted. Some were taken somewhere else and I never saw them again."

"How many were there total and how many disappeared?"

"Twenty-four and six were taken."

"What happened to the rest of you?"

"We were regularly interrogated, fed, and put through a bunch of medical and physical tests."

"Interrogation, as in torture?"

Her father leaned forward, clearly eager to hear her answer.

"Not everyone."

"But you were?" the agent asked, reading between the lines.

"Yes," she said. "But I wasn't supposed to be."

"What does that mean?"

"Their king ordered me not to be harmed. One of his men

didn't listen. Eventually, they assigned someone new to interrogate me."

"And the torture stopped after that?"

"Technically. I almost drowned one time during a test."

Her father narrowed his eyes. If the agent didn't press more on the subject, she knew he would once they were home again.

"Is there anything else you can tell us about your time there? What were they like? Do you know what they have planned?"

"The king forced me to eat meals with him." It was true, but saying it out loud felt like a betrayal of whatever messed up relationship she had formed with her captor. Maybe it was Stockholm syndrome but could someone experience that and still hate what was done to them as much as she did?

"Did he force you to do anything else?"

Her father shoved back his chair and began to pace the length of the room.

Verity caught his gaze and held it as she answered truthfully. "No."

She saw some of the tension leave her father's face but he wasn't relaxed by any stretch of the imagination.

"How were you able to escape?"

"I fought a few guards but then the king called them off and let me leave."

Mr. Kaur's eyebrows raised in surprise. His chauvinism was getting really old.

The doctor's eyes, on the other hand, lit up with approval of Verity's actions. The frown pulling down the edges of her mouth indicated she shared Verity's annoyance with their male seat neighbor.

He put down his pen and stared at her incredulously. "Just like that?"

"I did have a hostage with me."

The special agent glanced at her father for confirmation, as if he couldn't believe that she had fought off anyone—much less multiple alien guards. Her father nodded.

"They weren't going to risk killing one of their own," she added.

"Why not?"

She shrugged. "Aside from the guy who tortured me, they seem very loyal to each other."

"I see." He picked up the pen again. "And who is this hostage you took with you?"

"He was actually a mole here who used to be my friend," she said, leaving out the part where he was also her first.

Her dad would sooner commit murder if he knew that than leaving him alive to be interrogated and maybe even experimented on.

"What happened to him?"

"He's been taken into custody," her father answered.

"I'll need to question him, too."

Her father nodded.

"Who drove the ship back?" He gave her a bold once over, though at least he didn't look under the table to look at her legs. She would've kicked him in the face if he had. "I'm assuming you don't have space pilot training."

She bristled. He was right, but his assumption still pissed her off. Especially after he had already been forced to believe that she had fought off guards. She was perfectly capable of a lot more than he would ever give her credit for.

"Captain Tenner and an ASE scientist, who he broke out, handled navigation after we forced Trohm to cooperate," she begrudgingly answered.

"Forced?"

"They used a truth-telling serum on us at every interrogation. Captain Tenner managed to grab some."

"It's with the ASE scientist being analyzed right now," her father interjected.

"You mentioned medical tests," Mr. Kaur said. "What were they?"

"I don't know anything aside from what they used to test me. They drew blood one time and during every stress test, they put sensors on my body. I don't know what they were looking for."

He nodded as he finished writing. "That's all for now. I'll be in touch if I need any more information. Thank you so much for your time." This time, he addressed her before her father, but she could see a condescending gleam in his eye as he regarded her. He tucked the pad and pen back into his jacket and rose to leave.

Her father escorted him out, leaving her and the doctor alone in the conference room.

VERITY WATCHED the woman twirl her pen between her fingertips.

The pad in front of her had some writing on it but not near as many notes as Mr. Kaur's by the time he left.

"I don't mean to be rude," Verity started, "but can you tell me why you're here? I already have a primary care physician."

"I'm not here for your physical health, Miss Landau."

She flinched at the name. It brought back memories of Eiz'm.

Dr. Hudson noticed. "Would you prefer I call you something else?"

"Verity is fine." She'd told Knox that only friends were allowed to call her by her first name. And though she and the doctor weren't friends yet, she had a feeling they would be. Especially if the woman's annoyance with Agent Kaur was anything to go by.

"Verity, then," the woman confirmed. "Like I said before: I'm not here for your physical health, but to help your mental well-being."

"You're a shrink."

She smiled and didn't seem offended by the derogatory term. "A psychiatrist, yes."

"I don't need medication."

"We don't know what you need yet. I'm still getting to know you. Now, you told Agent Kaur," she said the name with enough disdain for both of them, "what happened but you didn't talk about what you were feeling while all this was happening to you."

"Like what?"

"Were you anxious, scared, irritable or angry, paranoid—"

"It's not paranoia if it's real."

Dr. Hudson nodded. "Point well taken. Now, did any of these or some other emotions apply to your experiences?"

Verity shrugged. In truth, it was all a jumbled mess. The answer was probably all of the above. "All, I guess."

"That's a good start. At least you can identify what you were feeling."

Verity rolled her eyes before she could stop the impulse.

"Other people who have been in your situation—"

She raised an eyebrow in challenge. The only other people were her fellow captives. Was Ben also receiving therapy? She doubted her father was forcing it on him like he was on her.

"People who have been captured and escaped of their own accord," Dr. Hudson amended, "sometimes have a difficult time identifying and articulating their emotions, which hampers my ability to help them work through them one at a time."

"What's the point? I'm home and I'm safe."

"I get the impression that you don't feel safe. And until you do, you can't live a fully happy life. I assume you would want that for yourself."

Damn, this woman was good.

Verity nodded.

"Good. Then I recommend therapy sessions three times a week to start."

"That's excessive." And while she was flattered that her father had thought of her mental health by arranging for a therapist, being forced into more sessions. There might be no physical torture but having to dredge up her feelings about the whirlwind of her summer? No thanks.

"Verity, I need you to trust me to do what's best for you. After some sessions, we can discuss cutting it down to two a month. Your father said we can meet here." She reached into her pocket and handed over a business card. "I also want you to know that everything we discuss together is confidential. No one here will know, not even your father, if you don't want them to. We'll be talking about your emotions, so the government can't compel us to break HIPAA laws or breach our doctor-patient privilege. If you have any questions, you can call or text me at the number on my card. It was very nice meeting you, Verity."

"Likewise. I think."

"That's perfectly understandable. I'll see you in two days." She stood and waited by the door.

Verity unlocked the door and found her father waiting in the sitting room. He stood at their approach, a silent question in his eyes.

She gave a small nod and the three of them walked out together.

Maybe it would be worth trying another session. The first one hadn't been so bad. And if it got to be too much, certainly she could convince her father to drop it. So, what was the harm with continuing the experiment?

Once Dr. Hudson had gone on her way, she turned to her father. "You don't have any more meetings today?"

"They're not until later. Time zones and all. I'll come back. For now, let's just go home."

Which meant he'd be talking to the secret space fighter programs of other countries. It was the one topic where map borders didn't get in the way of progress. It wasn't like the Race to Space or the Nuclear Arms Race. Killing each other was less important when their whole species could be wiped out.

"No fires to put out?" she asked.

"There was a custodian who took some unauthorized photos of your return."

"And?"

"The photos have been confiscated, he's been dismissed, and … *advised* of how to behave even though he is no longer employed here."

Verity suppressed a smile and didn't ask anything else on their way back home.

4

KNOX

KNOX HADN'T FORESEEN A VERY important factor in his plan to buy new clothes. Wearing his suit full time would be pointless as he had no enemies on this planet. And though Eochronian technology was much more advanced than that of humans, continual use of something still did result in wear and tear. And there was no need to subject his battle armor to that if it was unnecessary.

Which meant he needed clothes to fit in. And he needed human money. His mole, although very successful at his job, was unfortunately not paid enough by the humans in order for him to have a lot of spare cash lying around.

As he left the house, he considered his options.

He could steal money easily from any location that held cash in a cash register though he preferred to avoid violence if possible. Being invisible while stealing money would likely eliminate the violence issue—people could not fight what they couldn't see, after all, should the robbery be discovered, news of the strange occurrence could spread. It would only bring attention to him because even if he remained invisible the whole time, once Verity heard about it, she would know he was nearby. But he couldn't let that happen too soon.

Which left persuading someone to give him money the same way he had gotten his ride. Though convincing someone to part with their hard-earned money would likely be more difficult despite the fact that the first situation involved one's personal safety.

He shook his head at the foolishness of their misaligned priorities that placed currency above one's own life. They had no idea the level of luxury they enjoyed by not worrying about their species' population. A potential loss of life—even their own—could be dwarfed by short-sighted desires and motivations.

He slipped the door key into his pocket and turned his armor invisible again as he slipped out of the house unseen. He hadn't yet decided if he would return in visible form but if he did, he would need to open the door with the physical key in case someone saw him in person or on a neighbor's security recording. Despite its close proximity to the secret air base, there wasn't any military security surrounding the homes. Perhaps to avoid garnering attention to the fact that some of their employees didn't live on base and were more vulnerable to being attacked. At least, by human enemies. The humans in both locations were both equally ill-protected against his forces.

Rather than conning another human into driving him, he decided to sprint toward his destination, a famous and infamous hub of human activity, following the directions projected inside his helmet. He arrived in moments and stopped short before he was mired in the crowds of people.

As he approached the Vegas Strip, he turned off the invisibility feature and projected normal human clothes again, this time, a little shabbier so his plan to play on human's pity would be easier. No one would want to give him money if he appeared super polished, which would make his job of convincing them that much harder. Best to remove all the predictable barriers before they became problems.

He slipped into a crowd walking towards one of the large

buildings with multiple signs advertising clothing shops. But first he needed to find someone willing to give him money. He turned his head slowly, scanning for potential targets. As an Eochronian, he was taller than the average human but he wasn't the tallest of his kind either so he couldn't see over everyone's heads. That honor used to belong to his father and was now held by Aerue while the *largest* was Dhaca. What Aerue lacked in breadth, however, he made up for with agility and strength. Knox might be smaller than both of his top guards, but he was fully capable of defending himself. His father had been a peaceful king, but his grandfather had insisted he start learning combat while he was still a child, even by human-year standards.

His attention was caught by a woman on the opposite side of the crowd, whom many were watching. It wasn't hard to understand why. She was scantily clad in a sheer leotard with glitter and feathers covering her intimate parts. She had sparkles applied to her eye lids and cheeks, making her almost glow in the summer sun. Her blonde hair was pulled back, with a glittering feather headpiece holding it in place. It resembled a peacock, if he wasn't mistaken.

Interest lit her eyes as she looked him up and down. He smiled. She didn't have any place store money on her that he could see but maybe she could be useful. She was already receptive to him without having to exercise his special ability.

He pushed his way through the crowd until no one stood between them. She blushed and motioned for her friend to come over. The second woman was a brunette and wore a matching outfit and expression as her partner as she took him in.

If he were vainer, he'd say it was because he was the handsomest Eochronian, but that wasn't strictly true. From what his spies had told him, most humans found their kind incredibly attractive and charismatic. He bet they wouldn't consider Eiz'm the latter, but he was an outlier.

Even Verity hadn't been able to hide her attraction toward

him, though she was the only person who seemed to want to fight it.

The only reason the woman in the car had hesitated was due to a healthy instinct for self-preservation.

"Can we help you, stranger?" the first woman said.

"I was robbed on my way here, and I don't have any money to buy new clothes for my friend's engagement party." It was a fancy enough event for humans that he could get a suit without being questioned. "There's probably nothing you can do but if you have any ideas of how I can make money today, I'd greatly appreciate it."

"Well, gambling is out," the brunette said.

"Do you have any marketable skills?" The question was benign, but the tone made it very clear the line of work she was considering for him.

He shrugged. "I can heal people."

Both of their eyebrows shot up in surprise.

He chuckled. "I'm more than a pretty face."

Many people had drifted away during their conversation once they realized the women were only paying attention to him but those who were still lingering must have heard his words because they pressed forward and started shouting requests at him.

"My neck is really tight."

"My legs are always sore.

"My back is killing me."

Knox turned and smiled at the small crowd. He motioned them to line up and attended to each of them. For the neck, he merely sensed where the knots were based on the heat given off by the tightened muscles and focused his massage there. For the legs, he actually focused on the back, and for the back, he focused on the neck and shoulders.

Each person tested out how they felt after he finished with them and exclaimed in some way or another how much better they were now.

The brunette cleared her throat, briefly drawing attention away from him. "Well?" she said. "Pay the man. We all have to make a living, after all."

There were some murmurings as people did just that, and he graciously thanked them. Mentally counting, he had already made close to one hundred dollars just from those three simple acts.

Before more people could ask him to take care of their problems, he spoke up, "I'm not a masseuse or a chiropractor." He was very glad he knew the terms even though they hadn't come up often in his moles' reports. "I'm talking about bigger things."

"Like what?" the blonde asked him, touching his arm to get his attention again.

"Serious illnesses."

"Cancer?" Someone asked from the crowd.

"Blindness?"

"So... you're a modern-day Jesus?" someone asked. The voice was smaller and higher than most of the others.

He turned around and saw a young girl holding a teddy bear in her arms. A man stood behind her and was glaring at him. Her father, probably.

He knelt down until he was eye-level with her. "I suppose so."

"Blasphemy!" A voice shouted.

He turned and saw a man in black with a white collar. A clerical collar, if he was remembering correctly.

"I can prove it," he said.

"Do not let this poser sway you from the power that is Our Lord and Savior Jesus Christ."

Some people turned away from Knox turned to listen to the newcomer but many of their expressions were ones of annoyance. He doubted any of them were taking the man's words to heart.

He was proven correct when a few moments later, they all turned back to him.

"Where can I find someone to heal?" he asked the group.

"If you're working miracles, don't you have to do them for free?" the brunette asked him.

He supposed so. "I'll find another way to make money." He just wasn't sure how yet.

The blonde cleared her throat and the men in the audience turned their attention to her once more. "If this man can do what he says he can, I propose we buy him a new wardrobe to help him on his way. Everybody who agrees, say *aye!*"

A chorus of voices did just that and Knox smiled.

The little girl tugged at his hand and he knelt down again to give her his full, undivided attention.

"Yes?" he asked. "Can I help you?"

She nodded but didn't elaborate.

Her father stepped forward and placed a hand on her shoulder. "She has stage two cancer. It was just diagnosed and we're about to start chemotherapy."

Knox searched his memory for the meaning of the term. Finally, it clicked. It was an incredibly strong method of treating the awful condition with unfortunate side effects that could weaken the patient to a dangerous degree depending on how long the treatment lasted. He could help this little girl. And he would.

"Where in her body is it located?" he asked the father.

"Her brain." The words were choked.

Knox nodded. That made it easier for him to heal her with an audience. He motioned her to step closer, which she did without any hesitation.

Gently, he placed one hand on her forehead and the other behind her head. No one could see it, but he activated the vibration detector of his suit to find exactly where in her brain the tumor was located through something akin to echo location. His invisible helmet showed him an infrared holographic diagram of the girl's brain.

Once he found it, he changed the vibration frequency to one that could break up and disintegrate the cancer cells, and the DNA contained in them. The vibration was too light for a human to feel the full weight of its powerful effects but the girl started laughing, startling her father.

"What's wrong?" the man asked.

"It tickles, Daddy," she said.

The man looked back at Knox, an eyebrow raised in question.

"It's normal," he assured the human. In reality, he had no idea. He'd never done this to a human before though he knew from the physics that it was possible. And laughter was better than the girl gritting her teeth or crying out in pain.

After a few moments, which was more than enough time for the cancer to be eradicated, he switched the frequency back to the first to double-check.

When it came up clear, he smiled and sat back on his heels.

"Is that it?" the man asked.

He nodded. "How do you feel, sweetheart?"

The girl smiled. "All better now!"

"What do you mean?" her father asked.

"My head feels lighter!"

"What do you mean?"

"It doesn't hurt back there anymore."

Some people pressed closer but Knox gave them a warning look, and they backed up, giving the girl and her father some space.

The naysaying priest from earlier spoke up. "We don't know that this charlatan's trick worked."

The father crossed his arms and stepped up to the man, towering over him. "Are you calling my daughter a liar?"

"No, sir. But we must be wary of false idols and saviors."

No one listened to him.

"Me, next!" A woman shouted, pushing to the front, earning many glares.

The brunette in costume placed two fingers in her mouth and whistled loudly, causing everyone to freeze in their attempt to move to the front of the haphazard line that had been forming before him.

"We said we'd pay him after proof. He gave us proof. Now, put your money where your mouth is, ladies and gentlemen!"

While people started reaching for their wallets, he made eye contact with the woman and sent her a wink.

KNOX WALKED THROUGH THE MALL, taking in the different window displays as he passed them. There were a shocking number of technology-based ones for what had been advertised as a clothes shopping center. If humans hired game designers and developers to create weapons, they might be closer to being able to have a fighting chance against Eochronian technology but as it stood, the vast majority of their cutting-edge technology was only relegated to the imagination.

As he moved through the hallways, some people turned to give him passing glances, but not nearly as many as he'd received on the Las Vegas Strip. Though, he hadn't been the only cause in that instance. It was also partially due to the attention-grabbing women he'd been standing nearby.

Extricating himself from them and the people requesting him to work miracles on them had been an entertaining ordeal, but he was glad to be free of their scrutiny. And it wasn't all bad. They had collectively paid him five thousand American dollars for his time. He doubted he would need it all and would likely give it to his mole, as a sort of rent payment, though the idea was laughable given said mole was living there at the government's expense.

He walked into a store filled with suits. A man wearing the same suit as one of the window mannequins approached him. "Is there anything I can help you with today, sir?"

"I'm looking for a suit I can wear casually but also to some nice events."

The man nodded in understanding. "Of course. Please follow me."

They went toward the left side of the store where a collection of varying shades of gray, dark blue, and black suits hung on racks.

"I think you'll find what you're looking for here. If you need assistance, you can click this," the man gestured to a button on the wall labeled *call an attendant*, "and someone will come to assist you."

"Thank you."

Knox began sifting through the options, trying to find one that reminded him of his usual garments. He might be blending into humanity but that didn't mean he was going to forego all aspects of his true nature.

And, in reality, he'd worn something similar during his meals with Verity to make her more comfortable. And her reaction had certainly been favorable on those occasions.

He could practically still feel her hands gripping his jacket as she kissed him.

He smiled at the memory. He couldn't wait for it to happen again. From his moles' reports, her transformation was still in effect despite her being back on Earth. She should start realizing something was different very soon if she hadn't already.

Returning to the current moment, Knox selected a lighter gray and a dark navy, one in each hand. He then held them up to himself and glanced at the mirror on the far wall.

They both seemed well-sized for him, but he wanted to be sure.

Before he even hit the button, a female attendant stepped around from one of the racks and greeted him. "Is there something I can help you with, sir?"

Clearly, the people here were trained to start with the same sentence. Though her inflection was more similar to the costumed women than the man who had first helped him.

"Where can I try these on?"

"The dressing rooms are right this way." She gestured to a sign on the other side of the store and while he could have easily gone on his own, she escorted him to the door and hesitated before leaving him alone.

Knox quickly dressed and was pleased to see he had been right. They fit perfectly. He changed back into his armor with its facsimile of human clothes, and went to go pay for his clothes.

After a few more stops, he had a full wardrobe that would allow him to go unnoticed by any human except one particular female who would no doubt be on the lookout for him.

5

VERITY

THE NEXT MORNING, Verity zipped up her bag and slung the strap over her shoulder as she made her way down the stairs.

"Where are you going?"

She turned and saw her father emerging from the kitchen, his arms already crossed and braced for a confrontation.

"To college." She pulled the scrunchie from her wrist and drew her long hair back into a ponytail. "I already missed the first week back from summer break."

He caught her arm before she could reach the front door. "You're not leaving here."

Verity shook out of his grip and stared at him. "What do you mean? If I just stop going, I'm going to fail out of my program."

"It's not safe for you out there. I already called them and got you an indefinite leave of absence."

"People are going to think I got knocked up or something!"

Her father blanched, and she didn't miss his almost instantaneous glance at her abdomen.

She had the sudden urge to gag. She dropped her bag and ran to the bathroom.

He followed her and held her hair back as she threw up. She

hadn't even had the chance to eat breakfast yet so the acid burned her throat on the way back up.

"Are you?" her dad asked, his tone surprisingly calm.

"No!" At least, she didn't think so. They'd done a ton of things to her on the ship but they'd never done anything that could make her pregnant without her knowledge... right? And didn't the aliens procreate the same way as them? She'd assumed so based on when she had caught Knox and Arfilmea together but maybe that was for fun and not for biological reasons?

She sat back on her heels and flushed, a headache now pounding insistently behind her eyes. A migraine was *so* not what she needed right now. It was never welcome, but even less so when her world was falling apart at the seams.

"You're staying home," her father insisted, escorting her back upstairs to her bedroom.

She sat down on the bed with so much force, she bounced lightly. "What the fuck am I supposed to do now?"

"Language!"

"Really? That's what you're focusing on?"

"You're staying on base. It's safer here."

She opened her mouth to retort that the aliens had already broken in twice but shut it before sound could escape. It wouldn't really help her case. He'd probably put her under house arrest if she pointed it out. And she didn't need to lose any more freedom. She was done being cooped up.

"You never answered the question. What am I supposed to do if I'm not at school?" she repeated.

"Combat training."

"I've already taken the classes."

He pinned her with a hard stare.

"You'll take them again until I know you can defend yourself."

"When will you know that?"

"When you can beat Ben."

"Are you kidding me?" she exploded. "What about dance? I can't be fighting all the time."

His gaze flicked over her shoulder to their living room. "I'll get you a barre."

"That's not the same as being in class."

"You'll make it work. And you'll have guards."

"I'm not some maiden in a tower. I don't need a guard every second of the day."

"Of course, not. When I'm home, it'll just be the two of us."

"And the rest of the time?"

"I promise they'll be discreet."

That wasn't the problem.

"Who will it be?"

"Chapman and Davies."

"Not them," she said. Those two STFs harassed her every chance they got unless Ben or Tristan—Trohm—were ever around. They didn't care that she was the General's daughter. She didn't need them making comments about her body while she was dancing.

"What's wrong?"

"Just not them, please."

Her father's eyes took on a murderous gleam. "Have they done something to you?"

"They haven't done anything like what you're thinking. I would have kicked their asses. They just constantly harass."

"They'll be getting demoted."

She didn't argue.

"Then Tenner and Harrison."

She smiled. He refused to call Ben by his first name. Doing so would show favoritism. But they both know he viewed him like a son.

"Not Tenner."

"Why not?"

"Just, not him either, please." She couldn't deal with him scrutinizing her every move. Their time in space had only rekindled her crush on him and she needed distance from him. "Nothing is wrong, Dad, but please pick someone else."

He sighed. "Do you have a problem with McDonald?"

She shook her head.

"It's settled then. Harrison and McDonald will be your guards at all times."

"But do I still have to be stuck on base?" Before he could argue, she pushed forward. "What if they came to school with me? Before you say no," she rushed on, "one of them could be in class with me while the other stood at the door. I wouldn't try to slip away." Why would she? She wasn't a rebellious teen anymore. Wasn't she due some independence as a twenty-two-year-old? But even if she was, her father clearly wasn't going to give it to her.

She waited for his answer. If he said no, there wasn't anything she could do.

"On a trial basis."

She sighed in relief. "Okay."

They'll be driving you to and from campus. You need to send Harrison your schedule so he and Harrison have it."

She stood up again, ready to go. "I'll wait for them at the gate." She wasn't going to delay her departure in case her dad changed his mind again.

VERITY WANTED to shrink into nothingness as she walked through campus, earning curious glances and a lot of unabashed staring from her classmates.

It was obvious why she was getting all this extra attention, despite her father's assurances that her two guards would blend in. The two hulking STFs weren't exactly indistinguishable from her college classmates.

They were wearing t-shirts and jeans instead of their normal camouflage uniforms which only showed off their muscles to the female and gay population's great enjoyment.

But the guys didn't care, instead, they were intently scanning everyone around them to identify potential threats. She'd already given them a description of Knox and Aerue so they knew what they were looking for. So far, no one was setting off anyone's internal alarms.

She'd always had the uncanny ability to know when Knox was watching her anyway so having Harrison and McDonald with her were more of a precaution than anything else, and a bit overkill at that. Not that she could tell her father that.

And if the alien king tried to capture her again, having them defending her certainly couldn't hurt.

One of her friends came up to her. Alfie had come to visit her on base once or twice so he wasn't as fazed as her entourage's presence as everyone else. "What's with the body guards? You get famous over summer, or something?"

She shoved him lightly.

"That's the only explanation I can think of for why you didn't answer *any* of my texts at the end."

She swallowed. "I, um, I had a technology hiatus. Very unexpected."

"Did your phone break?"

"No." She needed to come up with a lie, and fast. "My dad decided to take me along for an extended camping trip."

"You? Camping?"

"I didn't say I enjoyed it." But it would've been better than what had really happened. She grabbed his arm and the four of them started walking to class. "What did I miss?"

He started rattling off the different hook up statuses of their friends and how someone on campus supposedly hooked up with a pop star but given they refused to *name* said celebrity, no one was really sure if it was true.

Even if she hadn't been abducted by aliens, there was a good chance she wouldn't have known all the information he was giving her. It's not that she wasn't close to her friends from school but she wasn't as entrenched in their lives as Alfie since her life was filled with her father's STFs every moment she wasn't on campus.

She took her normal seat in the center of the middle section in the lecture hall. Not so far back that a professor would call on her to make sure she was paying attention, but not too close to the front that the professor would call on her because she was directly in his line of vision.

Alfie sat on one side of her while Harrison sat on the other. McDonald sat farther back and a bit on the side so he didn't have to turn around to see who was coming in and out of the double-doors.

If they ate junk food, she'd offer to buy them stuff from the vending machine outside during break but she'd have to buy them coffee instead. Being an STF didn't allow for junk food because the program assumed fighting aliens would require everyone to be in peak physical condition at all times, so that meant that while they got cheat days, the STFs rarely took advantage of them. No one was ever technically on leave like other squadrons could be in the rest of the military. The rule was they had to stay within a two-hour drive at all times because disaster could strike at any moment without warning.

When her father had said they'd blend in, she assumed they would at least pretend to be taking notes during the class but neither of them had laptops or notepads in front of them, earning some questioning glances from her classmates as they started filing in and taking their own seats.

Verity suppressed a yawn. While she had been greatly looking forward to this elective about abnormal psychology when she'd signed up for it, she wasn't interested in studying what she was now living or getting into people's twisted minds. Thinking about a whole semester studying what led people to commit crimes, in addition to the cultural misconception that *crazy* people were all violent—when in reality, the vast majority of mentally ill individuals were passive and peaceful—just made her antsy.

Alfie noticed, which meant Harrison did, too, but her father's soldier didn't say anything.

"Hey, are you okay?" her friend asked, placing a hand on her bouncing knee to stop it.

She was lucky the chairs didn't squeak in this auditorium or everyone would know exactly how on edge she was.

Maybe her father had been right to restrict her to base. There were a lot fewer unknowns there, though nothing was a guarantee anymore.

She must have stared at his hand too long, or maybe it was Harrison's not-so-subtle clearing of his throat that made her friend remove it from her leg.

She smiled. If Alfie weren't gay, she would maybe think it was a flirtatious move but she knew it was nothing but a concerned and friendly gesture.

She forced a smile, though she knew it wasn't too convincing, and hoped he didn't call her on it. "Fine," she answered. "Just have some excess energy I need to wear off, apparently." She changed the subject. "So, you told me about everyone else but did *your* summer have someone special in it?"

Alfie blushed. "Actually, yeah. But it's still pretty new and he hasn't come out to his family yet so we're keeping it on the DL for now."

"How do you feel about that?" Alfie was one of the proudest gays she'd ever met and had the good fortune of never having to hide that part of his identity. She had to imagine that hiding that part of himself, even if it were as a favor to someone he loved, would take a toll on his mental health.

He shrugged. "It's not ideal but I'm not going to out him."

"Of course not," she said. "What's he like? Is he a student?"

"Actually, he works for NASA."

"I thought you hated science."

"True, but he can talk stars to me all he wants. Stargazing is so romantic, you know."

She wouldn't if they were only counting personal experience but she certainly did based on romance novels and movies.

Verity smiled. "When can I meet him?"

"We only just met in person yesterday. But we've video chatted a lot before that. He travels every so often but he just got into town yesterday. He's staying with me. I don't know if I want to spring the friend group on him during our first meeting, though."

She shrugged. "Well, whenever you're ready for me to meet him, I can't wait. If he makes you happy and isn't creepy, that's what matters."

He smiled and they turned to the front of the auditorium just in time for their professor to turn off the lights and share the day's slideshow.

"ARE YOUR CLASSES ALWAYS SO BORING?" McDonald asked her as she walked out of the lecture hall.

Alfie chuckled and waved goodbye as he split off from them towards the library.

"Just because the inner workings of the mind doesn't interest you doesn't make it boring," she retorted. "But if you want something more active, I have dance later tonight."

"That's hours away."

"Do you always complain this much?"

"Only when our superiors aren't around to hear it," Harrison answered, earning a hit from his fellow STF.

Verity sighed. Honestly, they were all like little boys when there wasn't supervision.

"Please tell me you have something more interesting for your next class?" McDonald asked.

"Depends on what you consider interesting."

"Ha ha. You're such a comedian. Seriously, what is it?"

"Were you not paying attention to me *at all* when I ran through my schedule on the way here from base?"

"Hey! I was navigating."

Harrison snorted. "If that's what you want to call it."

The truth was, they were both giving McDonald shit. He was one of the youngest in the squadron but her father wouldn't have assigned him to her protection detail if he weren't fully capable of the job at hand.

"I have my writing seminar." She'd put it off last year and while she didn't regret the decision, she really wished she had already gotten it out of the way so she could've added a more interesting elective or extra studio space into her schedule.

McDonald made a snoring sound, then immediately cut himself off and stood at attention.

She made a quick scan around to find what he and Harrison were looking at but didn't see anything amiss. Just more classmates staring at them.

"What's wrong?" she asked.

"Seven o'clock," Harrison whispered.

She made a show of repositioning her bag on her shoulder and glanced in the direction he had said. Again, she couldn't figure out what had put them on alert but she straightened her spine and prepared to fight or take off if necessary.

"Move faster," McDonald muttered, ushering her forward as they all picked up pace.

Harrison went ahead and held the door open for her. They followed her and she flashed her student ID. They started to head farther in but the guard stood up and told them to wait. Before he could come out behind the security station, Harrison and

McDonald pushed their security badges against the glass with a coordinated sigh.

A moment passed before the guard waved them on.

"I thought the General called ahead," Harrison muttered.

"He's new," she answered. He had to be. She'd never seen him before.

Harrison picked up on her silent thought. "How new?"

"Since I was last here."

"On it," McDonald said, and pulled out his phone.

They sat down in the back of room. Her professor already sat at his desk and raised an eyebrow at her armed escort, even though their weapons were concealed.

She dropped her bag off on the chair between them and went up to her teacher to explain the situation.

Based on his expression, he clearly thought it was overkill but didn't argue.

Join the club, buddy.

By the time she got back, the guys were looking over the employment file and background on the guard up front.

"Any problems?" she whispered.

They shook their heads.

She relaxed into her seat, and pulled out her laptop. She glanced at the clock and suppressed a sigh. This was going to be a very long day.

BY THE TIME Verity made it into the dance studio, she was ready to drop.

At some point during the writing seminar, she started feeling nauseated again and had thrown up yet again in the bathroom. Harrison hadn't said anything when she reemerged from the women's bathroom where he stood sentry but she could see the question lingering in his eyes.

"I'm fine," she'd assured him as they had headed back to class.

She stripped off her top and her jeans, revealing her dance clothes underneath. Normally, she would've changed in the dressing room but knowing she was having guards today, there was no way she was going to embarrass herself amongst her fellow dancers by having them clear the dressing room while everyone was changing.

She tucked her clothes into her bag, put on her pointe shoes, and left her bag in one of the cubbies on the opposite side of the room from the mirrored wall.

Harrison was keeping his eyes dutifully off her but McDonald wasn't so good at hiding his interest. Whether it was actual interest in *her* or just the fact that she was wearing a tank top and leggings, it was hard to tell.

Her teacher walked in and immediately hit play on her iPhone, sending music pumping through the studio's sound system. She stood in front of the mirror facing the rest of the room, and Verity could tell the exact moment when she noticed Harrison and McDonald.

"I didn't realize it was bring your friends to class day, Verity."

Verity sat down on the ground and spread her legs into a center split to start her stretching.

She heard a choked noise behind her and watched the mirror reflection as Harrison elbowed McDonald in the stomach.

She'd always been told to do other stretching before going into that position but she'd never had a problem with it. But today, she could practically feel the individual fibers of her muscles stretching. The hyperawareness of her body was new since she returned home from space and it didn't seem to be going away anytime soon but at least she hadn't felt like she was going to collapse while walking around campus.

"Don't mind them," Verity said, giving her teacher a meaningful look that she hoped conveyed the directive to not ask any questions.

Her teacher nodded once but her gaze lingered. "If either of you boys would like to join in, I'm sure we'll find space for you."

Harrison politely declined. "We're good but thank you."

Her classmates filed out of the dressing room and joined her in stretching.

After a few minutes, the music's vibe changed from soft and relaxed to louder and more energetic to get their heart rates going as they did floor exercises.

6

KNOX

KNOX LOOKED DOWN from his perch up in the tree nearby the dance studio. It was a separate building from all the others with almost floor-to-ceiling windows. Partially blocking his view were two soldiers from the human airbase.

He smiled. He could easily take them out without a thought but he wasn't about to go after them right now. They were protecting Verity, and as much as he wanted her with him and entirely to himself, the safer she was, the better.

Knox still wasn't sure who had left a note supposedly from him, and if someone was acting rogue, he had no idea if she was safe. He knew Eiz'm would probably like her dead, and if he was giving orders, it was better that she had guards shadowing her. He would do his best but there was power in numbers.

He shifted so he could watch Verity leap diagonally across the room, her long legs extending forward and backward as she lifted into the air as if pulled up by a thread. Her toes were curled to create straight lines of the top of her feet and he couldn't help but wonder if her toes would curl during their lovemaking. He'd certainly be looking for it when they eventually got to that stage.

A good lover drove their partner out of their mind, and if her instincts were taking over, then he will have done his job.

Each time she went up, her cropped top lifted ever so slightly, baring a sliver of her smooth stomach. Her top also only covered one shoulder, leaving the other open to his gaze with a thin strap keeping that side up. And every time she landed between jumps, her feet came down lightly enough that nearly barely heard.

Despite her grace and strength, he could see tiny tremors in her muscles and a small line forming between her eyebrows. She was unhappy about something, and looked almost as uncomfortable in her body as she had when she had been in pain after her sessions with Eiz'm.

He wanted to give her more healing serum but the small amount he had brought with him on his trip was only good enough for his personal use in case of emergency. And if his suspicions were correct, the healing and pain-killing effects of the one he'd given her before wasn't what she needed, either.

She needed Eochronian nutrients, based on her blood test results from when they were aboard his ship.

He doubted the mutation had halted due to the change of environment and available nourishment but it was likely slowing down as her new Eochronian DNA and cells were starting to cannibalize her human body. She hadn't received treatment long enough for her to completely transition but like any virus and mutation, the body was fighting anything foreign it could find.

One of the men stiffened against the window and turned around, looking outside the window as dusk was starting to fall. He even glanced up at the tree but Knox was invisible so he wasn't worried.

The dancers cycled through the exercise a few more times until each of them had moved across the floor four times. Then, the group lined up against the walls, holding onto wooden bars that were connected to the wall.

Knox watched as Verity and the others started to move in sync, bending up and down, creating a diamond between their legs every time they dipped.

When they started bending forward and backward, and left and right, he was treated to a perfect view of Verity's lush backside and curves.

What he wouldn't give to run his hands over her right now. He adjusted his position and mentally ran through all the fight moves he had learned as a child until the fog of lust cleared from his eyes.

He couldn't let himself be overrun by his baser urges. Patience was what he still needed to exercise and he'd be damned if his first day on Earth broke a few millenium's worth of self-control.

But there was no reason to tempt fate.

He climbed down and was right in front of the window when he heard the one who'd looked outside tell the other, "I'm going outside to check something. Keep your eyes on her." He paused before he added, "On her face, McDonald. You hear me? We don't want the General killing you because you came on his daughter."

"Yes, sir," the man named McDonald answered, his posture stiffening.

Knox moved further away from the building and found himself face to face with one of the men.

Without a moment's hesitation, the human bravely threw a punch into the darkness.

Knox easily ducked but the soldier's aim had been surprisingly accurate for a pure human who was unable to see through his kind's camouflaging technology. There was no chance he was part Eochronian or they would have sensed it during their surveillance but he would be a strong candidate for their program once they widened their target population.

Another striking punch was thrown and Knox was tempted to grab the man and subdue him.

When a third punch finished with the man's closed fist a hair away from his nose.

His instincts kicked in and he grabbed the man's hand, twisting until he heard the tendons stretch just past their breaking point, then let go. He wasn't going to break the man's hand or seriously injure the soldier but Knox also wasn't going to allow the human to keep going until he eventually hit his target: him.

To his credit, the soldier didn't let out any sound of distress at the injury. And he didn't back down.

Instead, the man used his other hand to throw another punch.

Knox took a step back and was surprised when the guard didn't let hitting air deter him. No, the man kept advancing into the darkening night as they got farther away from the dance studio's lights.

No other buildings were nearby to illuminate the space. He was sure Verity's guards weren't pleased about that, but he assumed she had been too stubborn to give in. But he wouldn't be in this position if they had forced her home after her final academic class.

Apparently realizing his punches weren't effective, the man threw a kick that glanced off Knox's hip. It didn't hurt him, of course. It wasn't a strong enough blow to penetrate his armor, though he could tell that it was more powerful than the average human was capable of.

If this kept up, the man's partner would certainly come looking for him and the two of them would investigate.

His only option was to take the man out.

Before the man could attack again, Knox stepped inside his personal space head-butted him, then punched him in the gut so he doubled over, and slammed his elbow down on the back of the man's neck, sending him down into the dirt. He waited to see if his opponent would rise, prepared for another round, but he didn't. Knox took one last look at the man's unconscious form before he ran away, listening for anyone's discovery of his body lying face-down in the grass but heard nothing.

The night hadn't gone how he expected and it certainly could have been worse but he needed to do a better job of staying under the radar.

7

VERITY

VERITY DRAGGED the hem of her top upward and dabbed the sweat off her forehead.

Normally, she'd barely sweat during dance class—a mystery no one had ever been able to solve—but today, she was practically dripping. Just another thing that had changed since her return.

She glanced over at McDonald who was now resolutely not looking at her bared stomach and likely the bottom of her exposed sports bra.

Harrison still hadn't returned even though he'd walked out only fifteen minutes into the class. That was forty-five minutes ago.

Based on McDonald's frown, he was also concerned, but she had heard Harrison's directive to him to keep his eye on her the whole time.

Otherwise, it would've been safe enough for him to leave her as class continued inside as he checked on his buddy.

She went to her bag and dressed quickly, trying to ignore the icky feeling of having her sweat-soaked clothes pressed against her skin by the addition of her additional layer.

It was still summer but now that it was dark, the air was a little cooler and it was important she keep her worked out muscles warm. If they got cold too fast, they could cramp, and that was always a pain in the ass.

She swapped her pointe shoes for her sneakers. Once her bag was packed, she walked with McDonald to the door. He went first and came up short, causing her to practically slam into him.

A curse exploded from him and she jumped back. She'd never heard McDonald sound so freaked out or angry ever before.

Verity heard some of her classmates shuffle around and try to see what was happening but if she didn't have any luck right behind McDonald, there was no way any of them would be able to catch a glimpse of what was going on.

McDonald took a step backward, moving further into the studio and closed the door behind him. "Call your father."

"What happened?"

"*Now*, Verity."

She reached into her bag's concealed pocket and grabbed her phone. She was already dialing as she asked, "Can you tell me what's happening? You're starting to freak me out, McDonald."

He didn't answer her right away.

Instead, she heard her father in her ear. "Verity?"

"Hey, Dad." She hoped her voice didn't shake. She had no idea what was going on but she knew it wasn't good.

"What's wrong?"

McDonald held out his hand and she handed her phone over without a moment's hesitation.

"Hello, sir."

She could still hear her father on the other side. "What the hell is going on over there, McDonald? Harrison isn't responding to my request for a sit rep and now my daughter is calling me clearly upset. Do not make me come down there."

"I need backup, sir. How soon can you get someone to our location?"

"Is my daughter hurt?"

"No sir. She's fine. But it's an emergency."

She heard her father curse and then his voice moved too far away from the phone for her to hear him. If he was calling in reinforcements, he was probably using the intercom in their home or the secure line he had in his home study.

He eventually came back and said, "They're on their way. Now, are you going to tell me what this is about?"

McDonald met her gaze and she knew the answer before he spoke. "Harrison is dead."

She heard a gasp behind her and couldn't bring herself to look over her shoulder to find out which of her fellow dancers had let the sound out.

For all she knew, it could've been her teacher. It didn't really matter. She'd barely been able to choke down her own shock.

"I'll keep in contact via the earwig from now, Sir," McDonald said into the phone and ended the call. He looked at her teacher over Verity's shoulder. "Is there a back door out of this building?"

Verity turned and saw the woman nod.

"I need everyone to go out that way and to not disturb the area outside this exit."

Everyone nodded, dumbfounded, and started filing out in the opposite direction. Some of them looked completely numb to their surroundings while others were staring at her with a new light of understanding in their eyes, as if they were recognizing the danger her proximity posed to them.

He handed her phone back to her and she pocketed it into her pants pocket. That way it was *on* her if there another emergency.

"Can I see him?" she asked McDonald.

He shook his head. "It'll only upset you."

"How can it possibly be worse?"

He hung his head in resignation and allowed her to crack open the door and look out into the darkness. Despite the general lack of light, what she saw made her hands fly up to her mouth.

Strewn across the campus grass was his body lying face down… and his head at least a foot away.

"Oh my god," she breathed, unable to think of anything else to say.

She felt another urge to vomit and rushed to the bathroom, McDonald hot on her heels.

She tightened her ponytail as she ran, the dance class having loosened it with every jump. She didn't want it falling into the toilet as she bent over it. She'd already experienced that on her twenty-first birthday after partying with some of the STFs, an event to which her father had surprisingly turned a blind eye.

She heard McDonald open the bathroom door but he didn't come any closer.

"Didn't you do that earlier today, too?"

She nodded.

He gave her a studying look.

She held up a hand. "Don't even think it."

He shrugged. "Too late."

She turned her back to him and rinsed her mouth with water from the tap. She gagged again. Ugh, she needed toothpaste, but that would have to wait until she got home.

"Feel better now?" McDonald asked.

"As good as I can right now." Her mind was still reeling over the reality of Harrison's death. "How long until we can leave?"

He checked his watch and then his phone, likely tracking his fellow STFs' location. "Twenty minutes."

"What am I supposed to do in the meantime?"

He pointed to her bag. "Hydrate?"

She pulled out her water bottle and took a big swig, all the while reminding herself that chucking it at him would be an incredibly immature thing to do.

He hadn't done anything wrong. She shouldn't be taking out

her frustration on him. It wasn't as if he had killed Harrison, and he couldn't have done anything to stop it. He could have gotten killed himself and he had been following orders at the time by staying with her.

Which made it her fault more than anything, if the blame lay with a human, at all.

But it didn't, did it?

No. The blame lay squarely on one alien king's shoulders, and god help him if he ever came too close to her again. The whole base would be lining up to kill him and even that would be too good for him.

Taking her and the others for some twisted experiment had been one thing. But *killing* someone? Murder was murder, and definitely an act of war between his species and hers, even if he couldn't see how the kidnapping part had already been one.

This left no room for debate, and he would pay.

It was just a matter of time.

VERITY SAT at the kitchen table as her father paced back and forth. McDonald stood by the door and Ben was standing with his hip propped against the counter.

"And you didn't see or hear anything?" her father asked for about the millionth time, directing the question at both her and McDonald.

"No, sir."

"Dad, my teacher was blaring music throughout the whole studio. We probably would've barely been able to hear gunshots if they were right outside."

"Were there any?"

She gave him a look. "It was only an example, Dad."

Her father turned to Ben. "What have they found?"

"Some footprints starting from a tree outside the studio and leading away from Harrison's body, sir. They're following the trail but it disappears once the grass ends. I don't think we'll get anything from it."

"Follow it, anyway."

"They are, sir. I just wouldn't—" Ben cut himself off at the General's quelling glare.

Verity sighed. "I had no idea this would happen."

"I did," her father said. "And I still let you leave the base."

"Dad, worrying something was going to happen and *knowing* for sure—"

He let out a curse. "That could've been you!"

She stood up and stood in his path, almost getting mowed down by him in the process. "But it wasn't," she said, softly. "I'm here, and I'm safe. And I wish Harrison were, too, but he's not. It's not your fault, Dad."

"I have to tell his family."

"I can do it," she volunteered. It would be uncomfortable and sad but maybe it would help her get past the shock so she could actually and truly grieve his death. He had never been as close to her as Ben or Tristan—before she knew he was really Trohm— but she had always liked him as a friend.

"No," her father said. "It's my responsibility. But can we now agree that you're staying here?"

The question caught her off guard. She expected another directive, which would have been completely in his right, even more so than when he'd last done it during their argument that morning.

She nodded.

"Good. Tenner will be your guard."

"Dad!"

If she hadn't wanted Ben around as her guard before, there was *no way* she wanted him assigned to her when it was now abundantly clear that Knox was willing to kill to get to her.

And based on how little the two men liked each other already, it would only be that much worse.

"McDonald, if you don't object, you will continue your responsibilities."

If the young man was afraid, he did a good job of hiding it. His gaze was steady and clear, and she didn't see his Adam's apple bob nervously like she expected to. He looked her father in the eye as he answered, "Yes, sir."

"You'll both be staying here for the foreseeable future. Captain Tenner has already brought his essentials. McDonald, you go do the same now. You'll be staying in the guest room on the first floor. I'll leave it up to you to decide amongst you who will take the first watch. And if I find out either of you crossed my daughter's threshold outside of an emergency, there will be hell to pay. Understood?"

Both of his men replied without hesitation. "Yes, sir."

He nodded, dismissing McDonald for the time being.

Verity walked him to the door. "I'm so sorry about all of this."

He gave her a reassuring smile. "It's not your fault either."

"I know." Logically, she did, but her emotions were being a little more difficult in accepting the truth. "I'll see you later. Be careful out there."

"I'll be back in no time."

She closed the door and made a beeline for the refrigerator.

She saw veggies for her and her father's morning shakes but not much else in the way of ingredients for a good meal.

"Can we order in?" She wasn't up for eating in public around the other airmen and base personnel.

Word had likely spread all over the base by now that Harrison had died protecting her and she couldn't deal with everyone's curious, if not justifiably accusatory, eyes turned on her.

Ben and her father glanced at each other and proceeded to have a silent discussion.

"He's not going to poison me," she interjected. "We already know he wants me alive and safe." For what, she still wasn't sure.

"Captain Tenner, go to DFAC and make a plate for Verity, and get one for yourself while you're there. Contact McDonald and tell him to do the same for himself and me. I'll take some of everything."

"Yes, sir." He walked out and she heard the door close behind him.

Verity sat down at the table and tapped her fingers on the wooden surface while they waited for the STFs to return from the dining facility.

"So…" she started, now that it was just her and her father again. "How was your day?"

They both hated small talk but sitting in silence left her too much mental space to worry about whether McDonald and Ben were okay.

"Fine," he grunted. "I had to babysit that jackass CIA agent while he questioned Trist—" he cleared his throat. "Trohm."

They both knew that what he said wasn't strictly true. As the General, he easily could have sent someone else to oversee the interrogation but he clearly agreed with her that Agent Kaur was a pain in the ass and a bit slimy, and therefore needed to be watched.

"Did you learn anything interesting?"

"He has an unusually high pain tolerance…"

"Compared to a human," she finished.

Her father nodded.

"Have you tried the truth serum Ben brought back?"

"The ASE scientist—"

"Zeph," she corrected.

"Zeph," he amended, raising an eyebrow at her, "still has it for research. There's not enough for us to use it right now without figuring out how it works first. We may never get another opportunity like this to study it."

"Of course," she said. "But it could make Trohm more cooperative and help us more."

"I'll take it under advisement."

"Are you feeling okay, Dad? Aside from the obvious upsetting stuff."

"Perfectly fine," he said.

Part of her wanted to push but the other part didn't want to in case the dam broke and her father started crying or something. She wouldn't know how to handle it, and he wouldn't want to be caught in what he considered a compromising situation if Ben and McDonald returned faster than they anticipated.

There were always lines at DFAC but sometimes they moved faster than others. The new guards could arrive any time. So, she'd let her father stew a bit longer but she wanted him to know she was there for him.

It didn't have to be a one-way parent-to-child emotional support channel.

"I'm here if you want to talk about anything," she offered, knowing full well he probably wouldn't take her up on it.

"I'll keep that in mind," he said, his voice choked with emotion.

She lay a hand on his arm briefly, then resumed her tapping on the table. Life under house arrest was going to be hell, but at least it was a familiar one and was free of the torture she'd been subjected to on the spaceship.

Though, therapy might qualify as mental torture, depending on how her future sessions went with Dr. Hudson. The doctor would probably have a field day with the new jumble of emotions Harrison's murder detonated in her mind like a claymore mine.

She sighed. This was not the life she imagined for herself at twenty-two, but here she was. Jumping from one jail to another, with no control over her own fate. Again. She hated it, and she planned to change that. She just had to figure out how.

8

KNOX

KNOX HAD JUST LET himself back into the apartment when his helmet started vibrating. There was an incoming communication.

He double-checked to make sure all the shades were closed before he answered. Aerue appeared on the holoscreen of his helmet. It didn't give him the distance afforded by the communicator he used during his last call. He could easily switch the device used, but he didn't get a chance before his friend spoke.

"What were you thinking?" Aerue's voice boomed in his ears.

Perhaps keeping it to the helmet was a mistake. Knox felt the urge to pace but doing so would be useless since Aerue would merely follow him with every step. "And hello to you, too. And what is it I'm supposed to have done?"

Aerue visibly lost his bluster and returned to his stern demeanor. "You didn't kill Verity's human guard tonight?"

"No! Why would I? Besides, I wouldn't be so sloppy that you would have already heard about it."

"Well, someone did, and beheaded him. And now the human air base knows all about it. From what I hear, the General is livid and ready to kill anyone who looks at him or his daughter the wrong way."

He could only imagine. If Verity was anything like her father, the man must be a force to be reckoned with when angered.

"Good to know, but I didn't kill anyone today, much less a human. And you know murder isn't my style."

"So, you had no interaction with the victim?"

"I fought him—"

"Your Majesty—"

"He was somehow able to detect my presence and was very good at aiming his fists. I had no choice but to engage him. But I left him incapacitated, not dead. I promise I did nothing to expose my presence or our kind's existence on Earth any more than our last visit to the air base."

"And you didn't give the order?"

Knox gave his best friend and top advisor a look that he found himself using more and more often since one particular human female had come into their lives. "No. What do I accomplish by doing that? She only gets buried further under lock and key, and I wanted to see her again."

"I thought you said you weren't going to be reckless."

He rolled his neck, forcing himself to relax. "I'm not being reckless." He stood up and started pacing. "This is unacceptable, Aerue. Someone is acting without my orders, and is jeopardizing everything we have worked so hard to achieve."

"He may be operating under someone else's orders."

Aerue didn't have to name the culprit for Knox to know to whom he was referring.

"What makes you think that?"

Aerue looked uncomfortable.

"Aerue," Knox snapped. "I asked you a direct question that requires a direct answer. Speak."

"Eiz'm called a council meeting."

"He did *what*? What happened?"

"I don't know, Your Majesty."

"What do you mean you *don't* know?"

"I was barred from entering the throne room."

"Who stood in your way? *How* did someone get in your way?" Then the second half of Aerue's words registered. "He was in the throne room? Without my direct permission? And the council went along with his treasonous actions?"

"Dhaca. He had other guards with him. I was outnumbered."

Logically, he knew Aerue had made the proper decision to not engage but he was pissed it had come to that and that his Head Guard was ganged up on by the very people under his command.

Knox sighed and rubbed his temples. "Is there anything else you'd like to tell me?"

"The council members I was able to speak to seemed very agitated after the meeting. They held out on telling me what was discussed but I can only imagine what the topics were."

So could Knox. Probably more concern about his and Arfilmea's decision to postpone their wedding and the production of an heir.

"You need to get back here, Your Majesty. Now more than ever. You need to put your fascination with her aside and reassert control before it's too late and Eiz'm mounts a full-fledged coup. It's clear he's been gathering even more supporters than I was aware of. It's clearly not just a small splinter group of radical rebels. I'm sorry, Your Majesty. I've failed you."

"No, you haven't."

"But I have. I've failed you in keeping an appropriately discerning eye on the situation. I knew it wasn't good but I wasn't aware of the extent of the damage until today."

"I don't blame you, Aerue. I didn't understand the full depths of Eiz'm's depravity either. I don't hold you responsible at all. I'll deal with all of this soon."

"When?"

"I'll keep you updated."

He closed the connection before Aerue could ask him for more specific details because he still didn't have them.

What was his plan, exactly?

He couldn't stay on Earth indefinitely to await the arrival of his people, especially since Eiz'm was aboard his ship proactively furthering an insurrectionist plot against him. He wasn't going to allow the rest of his kind to enter Earth's atmosphere until the final stage of his plan was ready for execution. Otherwise, he would be subjecting his kind to bland human food for no reason, and that wasn't fair to anyone. Even his temporary plan to stay hidden wasn't a foolproof plan, as proved by his run in with Verity's guard.

And once he did, he couldn't exactly spirit her away back to his ship with him again. There was a chance they could be shot out of the sky on a fluke by her father's men and they would both die a painful death.

Unfortunately, it wasn't impossible to kill one of his kind. Difficult under normal circumstances but falling to the ground due to gravity from a planet's atmosphere was an almost guaranteed way to physically maim if not kill him. And if it were that severe for him, it was definitely enough to kill Verity.

He squeezed his eyes shut and blew out a calming breath. How had he found himself in such an impossible situation?

9

VERITY

VERITY STRETCHED and kicked her blankets off. Automatically, she walked across her room and turned off her morning alarm, cursing herself for leaving it on this morning.

Her eyes were still heavy, and her throat was killing her. She hoped it was just due to dryness but couldn't be sure when it was also paired with what was a sinus or a tension headache.

She *had* been clenching her teeth all night through stressful dreams, mostly of her discovering Harrison's decapitated body on a sick loop, but sometimes the head on the ground trans- formed into Ben's, which always woke her up in a cold sweat. And if she was able to fall back asleep at all, it would happen all over again.

Either way, she hadn't slept well, and if she thought she could get away with it, she would've crawled back into bed and pulled the covers up to her chin. But her father was due to come in any moment now.

Right on cue, the door opened and he poked his head in. "You awake?"

"Barely," she mumbled.

"Sleep well?"

"No. You?"

"Could've been better. You have combat class first thing this morning. Your smoothie is waiting for you on the counter."

"Thanks, Dad."

He closed the door again and she heard his footsteps retreat down the hall.

She stripped off her tank top and went into her adjoining bathroom to brush her teeth with one hand and detangle her hair with the other.

Once she was done, she went to her closet and got dressed in shorts and a t-shirt with the STF motto. As she ran down the stairs, she braided her hair and met Ben and McDonald downstairs.

"My dad already leave?"

Ben nodded.

"Meeting?"

He shrugged.

Verity grabbed the glass off the counter and took a big sip before putting it back down. "He said I have combat class?"

Ben nodded.

Verity took her water bottle out of the cabinet and filled it with cold water then stuck it in the refrigerator so it would be cold enough to give her the relief she needed after the intense workout.

She picked up her smoothie and took another large sip, eying the two guys over the rim. "When did you both wake up?"

"We took shifts."

"Who got stuck with the graveyard duty?"

"I volunteered," Ben said.

She stared at him. Why on earth would anyone *want* to be up so late? And it's not as if it were for a fun reason like being at a party or seeing a midnight showing of a new movie. This was to watch for potential attackers who might be sneaking in under the cover of night.

Definitely *not* fun. And she would know.

"Are you... both going to be joining me for class?"

She didn't really want her ass handed to her by Ben in front of everyone today, and though McDonald was being incredibly good-natured about everything that happened, she was worried that some pent-up aggression could rear its ugly head at her if they were to step onto the platform together.

"We are your escorts," McDonald pointed out.

She cringed. "Do you have to use that word."

"Would you prefer we call ourselves guards?" Ben asked. "I thought you'd feel like you were back on the ship. I know I would, if I were in your position."

Damn it, he knew her too well.

She tried to think of a different word but came up blank. Where was a thesaurus when you needed one?

"I guess escorts is okay," she finally conceded

Though she couldn't help but feel like she was stuck in an erotica threesome novel every time she heard them referenced as such—even if they were the ones giving themselves the title. And she couldn't exactly share that reasoning with them without dying of mortification.

The STFs might like bragging about their sexual exploits, even with her present, but Ben never did in front of her and as the baby of the group, McDonald hadn't felt comfortable doing that yet. Bringing it up now would only make him feel awkward around her and given the fair amount of time they'd be spending together. She wasn't about to throw a wrench into their easy dynamic.

"Do you need the instructor to take it easy on you today?" McDonald asked.

It wasn't an outrageous question. She'd told them honestly that she hadn't been feeling well during dinner last night—which they'd already witnessed, aside from Ben—through her multiple bouts of throwing up throughout the day.

And she still didn't know why for sure. Verity hoped to god it wasn't her father's off-hand guess of her being pregnant. She resisted the urge to lay a hand on her abdomen to see if she could feel some sort of alien baby growing in there. It probably wouldn't work anyway since even normal human pregnancy couldn't be felt so soon. It's not like she was in some paranormal novel where she would start showing almost instantly. But if she *was* pregnant, it would be with some unknown hybrid just like that story.

She shuddered. She never wanted to have anything in common with that heroine and yet, she might very well be going down that road all the same.

Verity pulled up the period-tracker app on her phone and noted that she was three days late. She took a deep breath. Not great, but when she was stressed, she sometimes a week late. No need to panic just yet.

"You okay?" Ben asked.

She locked her phone before he could see the screen. The last thing she needed was him to start asking questions, too.

"You're not going to puke again, are you?" McDonald added.

She almost laughed at his bluntness, but Ben's alarmed face made her choke the sound back as she swallowed it. "I don't think so," she answered as seriously as possible.

She jumped when Ben sneezed loudly.

Now that she thought about it, she couldn't remember him ever doing so around her. She'd never known him to suffer allergies or get a cold, either.

"Are *you* okay?" she asked him.

He ignored her question. "Why would you ask that?" Ben asked his fellow STF.

"Because Harrison—" he paused to swallow awkwardly before restarting. "Because Harrison and I took turns taking her to the bathroom yesterday." He addressed her. "You don't have a stomach bug, do you?"

"I have no idea. I've been feeling under the weather for a bit but I don't know what it is." She stared at Ben, who eventually met her gaze, then looked away.

She narrowed her eyes at him. Did that mean he was feeling the same way? Had the aliens poisoned them, after all?

"Well, whatever it is, don't give it to me. I wouldn't want your dad to demote me because I'm too weak to protect you."

Verity rolled her eyes and finished off her drink. She rinsed it and left it drying upside down on the rack next to the sink.

"All right. Let's get this over with."

VERITY WAS INTERNALLY CURSING up a storm as her knee dug into the ground. She didn't remember kneeling hurting so much before. The asphalt pad was hot and for some reason, her kneecap was more susceptible to pain than it had been in a while like when she had first started taking these types of classes.

Maybe it was nothing. She hadn't, after all, been to one of these combat classes in a long time. And she didn't spend a lot of time on her knees as a ballet dancer, though she had during her modern and jazz units which had been a few years back during her time in high school.

But combined with the way she'd been feeling since coming home to Earth gave her the sinking feeling her current discomfort was related to what they'd done to her in space.

The airmen next to her in the front row who were in the same position as her didn't show any emotion aside from interest or concentration as they watched the cadre demonstrate a grappling technique with Ben. Once the instructor had noticed Ben, he had wasted no time in pulling him up to the front while McDonald was standing watch at the back, keeping an eye on her and any threat that could come from that direction.

Though Ben was clearly focused on the cadre in front of him,

Verity knew that he was probably watching out of the corner of his eye for any threats coming from the opposite direction.

She, on the other hand, was both trying to focus on the demonstration and everywhere else around her. The end result was that she wasn't focusing on anything at all.

"Okay. Now it's your turn. Buddy up with someone. Landau, you're with me," the cadre said.

Just her luck. Verity sighed and rose to her feet without her hands. It was a trick she learned when she was three, in ballet. Though the STFs around her could do it, too, they always were more forceful, as if there was some unspoken competition to see who could push off the ground with the most power.

She stood opposite the instructor and braced herself for him to make the first move. Luckily, he had a tell that she'd picked up on after only three lessons with him. His front foot would shift weight from his heel to the ball of his foot in preparation of closing the distance to invade his opponent's personal space. It was a slight and almost imperceptible thing that most people wouldn't even know to look for. But as a dancer whose teachers had the eye of an eagle and would get on her case for distributing her weight wrong even an inch off, noticing it came naturally to her. It hadn't saved her ass most of the time, but sometimes it came in handy when she was working on defensive techniques.

Predictably, the tell made its appearance, and she took a few steps back and rotated to beside to avoid his first grab.

She moved lightly enough to make her dance teacher proud but there was a split second where she was afraid she had made a misstep and was going to twist her right ankle. The last time that had happened, she was in her second year of middle school and it was so bad that she had actually landed herself with crutches due to fracturing her right ankle.

And that was when she felt at home in her own body.

Now, she felt like a stranger, constantly having to test out her movements as if all her appendages were phantom limbs. She remembered a book from her childhood about two siblings who escaped a kiddie version of Hell but that once they resurrected themselves by reentering their bodies, they didn't feel right because the tether between their bodies and souls had been severed. It had been an interesting description when she read it but now, she was essentially living it.

And she hated it.

When she evaded the cadre's second and third attempts to successfully grab her, he spoke up. "Are we going to dance all morning or are you actually going to do something?"

She rolled her eyes and refused to be baited. They always made dance jabs at her specifically but she'd like to see these badass STFs try to do a grand jeté first, and then they could talk.

But the next time he went for her, she obliged his request that she do something more proactive. She rotated with him and grabbed his arm from the side, and yanked him toward her, knocking him slightly off balance.

He righted himself very quickly but at the same time, she moved to his five o'clock, pulling his arm backward until it was stretched out behind him.

She surged forward, her surroundings seeming to momentarily slow down around her as she grabbed her instructor's wrist. She pinned it to the base of his spine and hooked her ankle around his and pulled, sending him face down into the asphalt.

He grunted, and she let him go then jumped back and out of reach before he could grab her ankles in retribution.

If he was shocked, too, he didn't show it. He seemed a little impressed. "Good job," he praised as he jumped to his feet. "Let's see if you can do it again."

She stared at him, a little surprised that she'd pulled it off. The connection between her fighting mind and muscles weren't as rusty as she expected them to be. But even then, it was a simple move that her instructor should have knocked her flat on her back before she was able to reposition his arm in the first place.

She couldn't. He kept moving out of the way so she couldn't manage to nail the same maneuver for a second time. She got flipped on her back a few times for her troubles, earning a few chuckles from the other STFs who were clearly so good at the exercise they had time to also watch her.

She tried again and he used his other hand to counter-attack, hitting her opposite shoulder, making her losing her balance.

Before he could hook her foot again, she moved her feet so she was further away from him.

But he moved with her and grabbed her from behind, similar to how the aliens had that night. Her mind went blank. She knew her body was still reacting, especially when she drove her elbow back into his gut but mentally, she was frozen in fear and unable to change the outcome of the past and present.

He let her go but flipped her by hooking her arms through his and rolling her over him similar to a dance move she'd done with partners in contemporary dance class.

She gritted her teeth and rose to her feet once again with her hands guarding her face.

Her cheek had healed since Eiz'm had gone to town on it thanks to time and Knox's special serum but she didn't want another blow landing there and setting her back weeks.

This time, she grabbed his wrist and flexed it, then turned around so her back was to him and pulled, launching him over her shoulder.

She heard a pop a split second before he let out a sound louder than last time. And it wasn't a normal winded sound that came from when she successfully dropped a guy from taller than standing position. Instead, he sounded like he was actually in pain.

She let go of him and knelt down. "Are you okay, sir?"

He rolled to his side and reached around to cradle the shoulder she had targeted with her attack.

She barely held in the gasp when she saw his scapula sticking through his skin.

"Call an ambulance!" she shouted, garnering the attention of everyone else who immediately stopped their grappling and sparring.

Ben and McDonald stepped up to the platform and took in the damage, protecting her from both sides.

Ben pulled out his phone and called for medical assistance after muttering to McDonald to call the General to let him know what happened soft enough so only the four of them could hear.

Everyone was staring at her and all she wanted to do was disappear. A sarcastic part of her almost preferred the being kidnapped again to the way they were looking at her now.

Like a threat. A traitor. Someone who couldn't be trusted. Like maybe she was in league with the very creatures who had taken her.

She heard the siren blaring from the other side of the base and watched as the medics lifted the cadre and placed him on a stretcher before loading him into the ambulance.

She risked a glance at McDonald and Ben. The young STF wouldn't meet her gaze and instead stared off into the distance, probably feigning being an alert guard. Ben met her gaze but looked more serious than she'd ever seen him. She could read the message in his eyes as if they were tattooed across his forehead: *This is very bad*.

She sat down on the platform and hung her head in her hands, not caring any more that it was a sign of weakness. The headache from earlier was now back with a vengeance and she could do with a bottle of pain killers right about now. Maybe it would land her in a drug-induced oblivion, and she could pretend to pass this off as a horrible nightmare instead of a nightmarish reality.

10

KNOX

KNOX WAS in the middle of soaking in the warmth provided by the star's rays, thanks to the filter he'd constructed to save sunlight the same way his ship could in the event of a cloudy day, when he heard the door open. His host was officially home.

He sat up and walked into the entry way to greet his agent.

"Your Majesty," the man said, bowing immediately. His next words were directed at the floor. "I hope you have been comfortable in my home."

"Yes. Everything has been very satisfactory. You may rise."

His agent did so and removed his outer jacket and hung it up in the small closet.

"Where have you been spending your time?"

His agent offered a sheepish smile. "Boyfriend's place."

Knox raised his eyebrows and regarded his man. Even scrutinizing him now, he couldn't see any signs of amorous relations. Unlike humans, he didn't care about the sexual orientation of any individual, or who they might be taking to bed, but he was surprised by the news. "I didn't realize you were in a relationship with a human."

"It's nothing serious."

Based on the tone of voice, Knox had a feeling it was anything but. "I see," he replied.

"Should I break it off, Your Majesty?"

The hope in his voice clearly hinged on the possibility that he would say no. Which he did. "That's unnecessary," Knox said. "If you're happy, then I'm glad. Just don't let it distract you."

Aerue would be internally rolling his eyes if he could hear him saying the very advice he was constantly receiving now. It was a perfect example of how stating a reality was easier than living said reality.

Verity Landau's ability to burrow under his skin and invade his every thought was more than enough proof of that particular quandary.

"Do you have news to report?"

"The General has me visiting every day and working with their weapons designers and technicians to prepare them for our kind's eventual attack."

"Only if necessary," Knox corrected. It was yet another topic he and Eiz'm differed vastly on. Why create an antagonistic relationship without giving a peaceful merging a chance, first? Although according to Verity and her father's military base, they had already sacrificed that option.

He refused to believe so. His agents around the globe had yet to report that every human country was ready to fight them. It seemed only this one was on a war path for now.

"Anything else to add?"

"She severely injured an instructor today."

"How badly?"

His agent gave him a meaningful look. "Bones were protruding."

Knox winced. That sounded extremely unpleasant. "I assume it was unintentional on her part?" She might have liked to maim him and his men on purpose many times but she didn't strike him as someone who enjoyed violence on a regular basis.

And given it was an instructor, she probably felt guilty about it, too.

She'd never feel that way if she were able to injure him in a similar way. No, the little spitfire would probably be gloating and complaining that she didn't hurt him more.

One of these days, he might incite a fight with her just to see how good she was, though he'd do it before returning to his ship because Aerue would never let such a display of her potential lethal power to happen.

"How is the instructor?"

"In pain but he is on pain medication and expected to make a full recovery given time."

"And her?"

"Shaken. She was whisked away by her father and her guards."

He didn't miss the use of the plural noun. "Who is on her detail now?"

"The surviving man from yesterday and," he swallowed, "Captain Tenner."

Now, why did he have a feeling that would be the case? He started pacing, wishing very badly he could punch the human out of jealousy. For being able to be near her. For their close relationship. For her liking him as more than just friends, though he wasn't convinced the foolish human was aware of that particular fact.

"Did she request him?"

"No, Your Majesty. She specifically requested he *not* be assigned to protect her."

Knox stopped and turned to look at him. He hadn't expected that. He wondered why she would insist on a separation. They were so close on his ship.

"She didn't want what happened to the other one to happen to him."

"And how do you know this?"

"I installed listening devices when her father called me in to do a security sweep of you leaving your love note in her room."

What note? It was probably the same person who had framed him in killing her guard.

"Apparently, she could see you on camera. As a blur, but still—"

Even though it wasn't him she saw, her vision was clearly now superhuman, as was her strength. "Anything else noticeably different about her?"

"She's getting sick a lot."

"Sick as in—"

"Vomiting, Your Majesty."

"How is she reacting to the changes?"

"Well, she's pretty freaked out about the vomiting part. She's afraid she's pregnant."

An understandable concern on her end. It was a normal sign of human pregnancy but it wasn't necessarily one for Eochronian gestation. Some of his kind showed it as a symptom but not everyone did. Regardless, there was no reason for Verity to be vomiting as a result of possible pregnancy.

Her body was likely rejecting the human food her system was ingesting again.

He'd have to talk to Dr. Mak'en about the swift and severe effects. While the transformation was certainly an internal-to-external one that would eventually be permanent but as he could eat human food without an issue—something he'd done twice so far, with little pleasure due to the limited range of tastes found in their earthly nutrition sources—Verity and the other subjects should be able to, too.

Granted, she was the only subject to be changing at this high a rate and the only one to be eating genuine human food after having started treatment. Perhaps he was wrong in assuming they would be able to tolerate human food after the transformation.

An inconvenience, to be sure, but not a dealbreaker as his planet's agriculture and animals could easily thrive on Earth as easily, if not easier, than his kind. And that didn't even account for the humans wanting to kill his species while probably not caring at all if herds of vesseans were to start traipsing along their fields along with their planet's native livestock.

It would likely arouse curiosity but nothing like the aggressive reaction that was awaiting him.

"Your Majesty?"

From the tone of his voice, his agent had been trying to get his attention for a bit.

"Yes?"

"Now that she's going to have the Captain with her at all times, it may be harder for me to get close enough to hear information directly from her."

"If the General already has you in their house, doesn't he trust you?"

"Only to work, sir. When I stayed socially, he had the captain watch us. I couldn't get her alone."

"Would she open up to you if you could?"

"I believe so, Your Majesty."

"She trusts you that much already?"

"The escape certainly helped my cause."

Knox nodded. He assumed it would. He hadn't been anticipating Verity discovering Trohm's true identity but it had been serendipitous in a way, serving to further establish the innocence of his other agent.

"If you're unable to directly observe her, I assume you have a backup plan?" Knox asked, returning to the second half of his agent's statement.

"Yes, Your Majesty. I already planted listening devices in her home and her school bag. She's now restricted to the air base but I haven't been able to install our surveillance system everywhere, yet. I don't have any way to keep track of her when she's not at home. Yet." He added the last word in a hurry, as if he were worried about displeasing his king.

"What's your plan to remedy the blind spots?"

"I have yet to upgrade the security systems on the other side of the base. I'm to start that tomorrow."

"Upgrade how?"

"Improved heat signature readings."

They both shared a humorous look before his agent continued.

"And some better slow-motion capabilities but I've warned them it's prohibitively expensive so it won't be at top capacity that the humans are capable of but it might be enough to catch a glimpse of you, like she was able to see. It wouldn't be enough for them to find any of us but it is better than what they have now."

"You can't sabotage them more instead?"

His spy shook his head. "Her father is very smart and sharply observant."

"Like his daughter," Knox mused.

"They're very similar. I understand her mother died many years ago."

He'd known that based on the information Trohm had fed him but he hadn't thought it overly relevant at the time. Perhaps his agent's inability to be near Verity because he was near the father wasn't an entire waste. The more he could learn about what sort of person raised Verity, the better he'd be able to understand her.

"Keep me updated on him same as you were about her."

"Your Majesty?"

"Make the arrangements you need to have eyes on her at all times but I want to know everything you can learn about the General."

"Yes, Your Majesty. Is there anything else I can do for you?"

"Are you done working for the day?"

"Yes."

"Then I'd like to explore humanity more than I was able to on my own."

"Of course. What would you like to see?"

"I'd like to return to the Vegas Strip."

His agent's eyes shot upward. "You enjoyed your excursion, there, then? I thought it caused a bit of a fuss."

"It did, but it served its purpose," Knox said, gesturing to his outfit.

"Perhaps we should get you some more casual clothes, too, Your Majesty."

"I've been busy." Knox walked to the closet and revealed the collection of short-sleeve shirts and jeans he had also gotten for himself in addition to the suit he was currently wearing. He just liked the feeling of the suit on him more than the itchy cotton.

"Then I suppose we can just enjoy ourselves."

Knox smiled. "That sounds like a wonderful idea."

THE WOMEN from his first visit weren't present this time, which was a small blessing considering he was now with another of his kind. And he didn't want to draw attention to the two of them because what could be written off as beautifully unique while he was alone in a crowd of humans would certainly turn heads with both of them together.

"Where would you like to go, Your—"

Knox silenced him with a look.

How unexpected that he would almost mess up so egregiously but he supposed it wasn't entirely his fault. It was his agent's first time being in public with him on this planet.

The last time they had conversed, he had been able to speak freely without worry of being overheard by oblivious humans.

And while his last visit had proven that the large majority of humanity didn't heed the ramblings of a single person, if multiple people started talking about them, it could very easily garner the attention of the human air base, and get back to Verity and her father.

He was quite frankly surprised that his healing the little girl hadn't resulted in just that, what with all the people who had been there to witness his charitable act.

Knox picked a direction and started walking. "Where would you suggest?"

"Well, I would stay away from the casinos. There's no reason to gamble the money we already have."

"Why not?"

"Because it's a simple game of chance that is often stacked against the player, and while we could easily manipulate the system, that takes the fun out of the whole thing."

"Isn't the fun derived from leaving with more money than you had going in?"

"Yes, but the true design is to excite the human's through biology feedback loops so they will keep trying even when logic would dictate their chances of winning are very low."

"Perseverance in the face of futility," Knox noted, scanning the buildings around them for an interesting destination. "An idealistic point of view, if there ever was one."

"A romantic notion, to be sure."

"What about a show?"

"They can be expensive."

"I have money to spare."

"Well, isn't that great news for us?"

Knox turned and noticed a group of four men who had followed them down the less-populated side street.

He heard his agent curse, and he held in the urge to do the same.

Not because they were outnumbered. The fight, if it came to that, would inevitably fall in their favor, but engaging in one could easily draw the attention of other passersby.

He should have been paying more attention to his surroundings instead of letting his mind float away on the possibilities of adventure offered by the exciting human city.

"How can we help you?" his companion asked.

"Give us your money."

He made no move to remove the wad of cash from his inner pocket. "Anything else?" Knox asked.

"Your suit," one of the other men said.

"Ah," Knox said. "This is a mugging, then?"

"Don't act like you don't know what this is! Give us your money and suit *now*!"

Knox didn't let the man finish speaking before he lunged forward and grabbed the mugger by the throat, lifting him a few inches off the ground.

The other men drew weapons, mostly guns. His agent quickly disarmed them and flipped them onto their backs.

That left one man left, staring at the two of them nervously. The knife in his hand kept reflecting light because of how much it was shaking.

"Drop it," Knox commanded.

The human did, and let out a high-pitched yelp in fear as he ran away.

His agent turned to him. "Should I apprehend him?"

Knox released the other man, letting his prone form drop to the ground.

"Not necessary. As long as no one sees us, no one will believe him."

"True."

They stepped around the bodies and merged into the crowd that was walking on the street.

"So," Knox continued, "what show would you recommend?"

11

VERITY

VERITY WALKED BACK toward her father's office door, wishing she could open it. But he had locked her in. She paced as she waited for Dr. Hudson to arrive for their next session.

It was scheduled as an emergency by her father after she'd been unable to fully describe what had happened during combat class.

She hadn't *meant* to injure her instructor. Okay, that wasn't strictly true. She had wanted to but only in a manner that would allow her to win the match, not land him in the hospital.

And she'd never been able to do too much damage during fight classes before, only enough to get her attacker to release her and sometimes briefly put them out of commission. In real life, that was more than enough for most scenarios where the main goal was to escape and find help.

She wasn't training for the same goal as the STFs she trained with. *They* had to learn how to kill people. She only had to learn how to fight long enough to stay alive.

The door opened and she stopped pacing immediately.

Dr. Hudson smiled at her and closed the door.

Verity heard the click and the electronic locks engaging, securing the SCIF once again.

"Hello, Verity."

"Hello." She forced a smile. "Bet you didn't expect to see me so soon again, huh?"

The doctor returned the smile. "Very true. But for me to help you as best as I can, I need you to be as honest with me as possible. I understand that you are used to putting on a strong front—"

"It's not a front."

"Then how would you describe it?"

Verity stared at her nails and resisted the urge to pick at a cuticle. "Armor."

"Is it constant or do you ever let your guard down?"

"Well…"

"Being asleep doesn't count as letting your guard down," Dr. Hudson added.

Verity shrugged. "Not that I can think of," she finally answered.

The good doctor made a small humming noise as she wrote something down. She looked back up and held her gaze. "I understand you are used to not showing weakness, likely due to your upbringing and surroundings, but I want you to know that I won't judge you for anything. And you pretending to feel one way will only prolong your mental distress if we can't get to what's really bothering you. That also means I need you to not censor yourself because you think something is stupid, or pathetic, or silly, or otherwise not valid."

Verity dropped into one of the chairs around the conference table. It was only her second time meeting the woman and she was already getting a lecture about not behaving well.

It wasn't a usual experience, either. The doctor was right about her assumption that she was always perceived as strong, and that also included always following rules.

Dr. Hudson sat down on the other side of the table, and pulled out her notebook and pen slowly and methodically.

Verity wondered how many times she had done that before. Did it ever get boring? Listening to people constantly talking about their problems?

She watched the doctor's eyes flick to the chair next to her and realized her sitting with the table between them was a calculated choice. Whether it was to keep a professional distance or allow her a type of barrier, she wasn't sure. But she appreciated it all the same.

"I understand today's fighting lesson had some unexpected events occur?"

"You could say that."

"Care to elaborate?"

"I injured the instructor so bad he was rushed to the hospital."

The good doctor nodded as if she heard such news all the time. "And how do you feel about that?"

Verity sat back in her chair. She focused on the feeling of her neck leaning against the top of the back and making her spine as straight as possible. It wasn't comfortable but it kept her focused on the present and kept her mind from getting carried away with unhelpful thoughts. "Guilty... scared..." She paused. How could she express how she felt like a total outsider in her own home now that everyone had seen the amount of damage she could do unintentionally.

If she got angry, would she go all rage monster like the famous superhero? And would the ASE scientists lock her up to experiment on her? Just another curiosity the as a flipside or even complementary experience to what she went through on the space ship?

The doctor stopped writing on her pad, and looked up from the table, making eye contact with her. "You're thinking about something else."

Verity stared back at her, refusing to blink. "Yes."

"Do you want to talk it out? Like I said, self-editing isn't helpful. You can say anything that comes to mind."

Verity repeated how she was feeling in vague terms, stuttering a few times, which made her want to scream. Her mother hadn't been a strict stickler for grammar by any means but she had emphasized the importance of expressing oneself clearly with enunciation and appropriate word choice.

While she never would have judged someone with a stutter, Verity hated when she did it. It only happened when her brain moved too fast for her mouth or she was still trying to untangle her thoughts while speaking, like now. Her normal approach was to be silent until she knew what to say, but that clearly wasn't going to fly with Dr. Hudson.

At least Dr. Hudson wasn't recording the conversation.

"That's all understandable," the woman finally responded. She noted something down, then looked back up at her. "What is the worst-case scenario?"

"What?"

"If you are an outsider and they do end up experimenting on you, what does that mean? Is that the worst case scenario or does that lead to something even worse? I want you to follow the spiral and take me along with you."

"Aren't you supposed to *prevent* me from overanalyzing and catastrophizing?"

"Generally, you could say so. In reality, I'm going to help you stop yourself, but we need to pull on the knot until it unravels so we know the heart of the matter." She laced her fingers together on the table. "So?"

"If they experiment on me..." Verity swallowed, imagining being laid out on a medical examination table with scientists and their needles hovering over her like abstract art imagined alien abductions, "then it might mean something's wrong with me."

Dr. Hudson leaned back in her chair. "Wrong with you, how? Can you be more specific?"

"That I'm less than human."

"What about *more* than human?"

Verity stared at her.

"I'm only saying that considering the evidence that your strength has *increased* since your return. Wouldn't that qualify as superhuman?"

"I suppose."

"Does that change your fear?"

"No."

"Why not? I would assume you'd want to excel at everything you do. If you were given a biological advantage, wouldn't you be happy?"

"I don't want to be experimented on."

"Why?"

When Verity didn't answer, Dr. Hudson repeated the question.

"Are you going to keep asking me that?"

"Yes. Until I get an answer."

"What if I lie?"

"You could, though I don't think you will."

"I don't want to be seen as different. And if I'm an experiment, then I already am."

"And even if you're not experimented on? What would being seen as different mean?"

"I wouldn't fit in."

"Don't you already not fit in? You're not actually part of this..."

"Military operation," Verity finished. She had no idea how much the doctor had been briefed on and she wasn't about to spill the beans on what her dad did for a living. She'd already been forced to do that, and she wasn't about to *volunteer* the information given how crappy it made her feel when it *wasn't* her fault.

For all she knew, Dr. Hudson only knew that she had been

kidnapped and experimented on by other *humans*.

"Anything else happen?"

Verity sat up straight. Did the woman have psychic powers?

"I froze during fight training."

"Care to elaborate?" Dr. Hudson leaned back, as if giving her the floor.

"My mind went blank."

"Did you physically freeze?"

"No."

"I see."

"See what?"

"Were you able to notice that you didn't physically freeze in the moment or only in retrospect because I asked?"

"I knew in the moment."

"So, you had the awareness of simultaneously experiencing different realities in your mind and body."

"What does that mean?"

"Well, it's not full-on dissociation, which is a good thing. But you did clearly get triggered by something during class. Do you know what the trigger was?"

That was obvious. "Getting grabbed from behind."

"Did that happen the night you were abducted?"

"Yes."

"Were you mentally in the present when you were grabbed from behind during fight class or were you transported back to that night?"

"Both?"

"Simultaneously again or in quick succession?"

She shrugged. "I don't know. It happened so fast."

"Okay," Dr. Hudson said, making a note in her pad. "We can come back to that another time." She laid her pen down. "Is there anything else you want to talk about?"

"I didn't sleep well."

"Nightmares?"

Verity nodded.

"Not surprising." She wrote something down in her notebook. "What were they about?"

"My friend dying." She paused. "It's my fault."

Dr. Hudson wrote in her notebook again.

"We'll definitely talk more about this during our next session. Compounding your other symptoms with survivor's guilt cannot be easy. Would you like me to prescribe something to help you sleep?"

And lose even more control of her body? Hell no.

"No, thank you," Verity answered.

The woman stood and held out her hand for her to shake. "I'll see you again in two days. Please contact me if you need to talk before then. Day or night. And I'll get back to you as soon as possible."

"Thank you, Dr. Hudson."

Verity went to her father's desk to turn off the SCIF function and unlock the door, officially bringing their session to an end.

VERITY WAS SITTING between Ben and McDonald when Chapman and Davies—or as she liked to call them: Thing One and Thing Two—plopped down opposite her in DFAC.

"How's it feel?" Davies asked.

She regretted her words before she even said them."How does what feel?"

"Being the reason Harrison is dead," he answered.

"And the reason Wells is in the hospital," Chapman added.

Before she could answer, Ben growled, "Knock it off, you two."

They turned to McDonald, next. "It must be hard, protecting her when she's the reason your buddy died, huh?"

Verity silently cursed them and herself for talking her father out of assigning them as her guards. They would've harassed her, sure, but they would've taken the job seriously, and maybe one of them would've died instead of Harrison, who was too decent a man to deserve it.

She'd probably still feel bad about someone dying while protecting her, but she wouldn't be mourning the *individual* if it were Davies or Chapman.

Even thinking the thought was probably going to send her to hell but she couldn't bring herself to regret the mean-spirited sentiment.

"Shut up," Ben said. "You don't know what you're talking about. And if you know what's good for you, you'll keep your uninformed and asinine opinions to yourself before they make their way to the General's ears."

"What? The princess is going to tattle on us to Daddy?"

Verity slammed her fork down. "No. I'd land you in the hospital like Wells, but this time I'd be trying to, so you'll probably need a lot more help than him when I'm through."

They stared at her, finally silent.

Chapman looked a little scared and Davies looked like he didn't believe her and maybe wanted to challenge her but was wisely keeping his mouth shut. For now.

The five of them finished eating in silence. She ate faster than even before and out of the corner of her eye, she saw her guards doing the same thing.

She smiled. They were good enough at picking up social cues to do it without her having to ask.

Whereas the two dumb-asses in front of her wouldn't know subtlety or how to behave with anyone with an ounce of class if they were disciplined by a ballet mistress at the end of her rope like Verity had seen her fellow dancers. God, she'd like to see them subjected to one or both of them.

Her father had said that they would be demoted but she couldn't tell whether it had already happened. Their attitude towards her today was worse than normal but it could just be attributed to Harrison's death. Her bet was that if they had already been dressed down by her father, they'd be glaring daggers at her, not throwing weak and immature verbal barbs at her.

On their way out, Ben stepped away from her and McDonald to briefly speak to her father.

Based on his murderous expression, he was being filled on the meal's conversation.

Her father strode to the front of the large room where a large number of his STFs were currently still chatting and eating.

"It has come to my attention that people have been speculating and discussing my daughter behind my back. Now, I shouldn't have to tell you all how inappropriate that is but it seems that there have been some specific individuals who have taken it one step further and started harassing my daughter directly."

Verity brought a fist to her mouth and bit her knuckle to hide her smile.

"Chapman. Davies. Up front, now."

She watched the men dutifully march single file up to meet her father's disapproving figure. They lined up at attention, their eyes fixed on the wall behind her father.

"Your behavior is a disappointment to me and the Air Force. It's a disgrace to the rank of First Lieutenant. As officers, you are supposed to be setting an example of for the enlisted. As such, you are both being demoted to Second Lieutenant. That will be all," he said, dismissing them back to their table.

"Let this be a lesson to everyone," her father finished, addressing the whole room.

He didn't look at her once, but she knew that he saw her in the corner.

Ben walked back to her and ushered her out quickly with McDonald following directly behind.

Verity smiled. Lunch might have started out sour, but it sure ended sweetly.

VERITY STARTLED AWAKE to the beeping of her phone. She didn't even mean to fall asleep.

She glanced at her open door, half-expecting to see one of her guards standing there

She scrambled out of bed and grabbed the device to see a new text from Alfie lighting up the notification screen.

Hey, girlie, where you at?

She typed back, My dad pulled me out for the rest of the semester.

OMG! was his reply, followed by the emoji she dubbed "The Scream" based on its resemblance to the Edvard Munch painting. How did you score such a sweet deal? My mother would never. Want to trade?

She smiled. He had no idea what he was asking for. Haha, nope. He would probably think she wasn't willing to give up her "sweet" situation but, in reality, she didn't want to inflict her super bad and crazy life situation on her good friend.

Anyway, before I forget, I changed my mind.

About what? They had talked about so much stuff during her single day at school that it was hard to figure out what he was referring to.

I'm willing to give up some one on one time with my boyfriend so you can meet him. Want to meet me on campus after my last class?

That would involve leaving the base, which was an absolute no-go with her father. Would it be possible for you to come meet me on base instead?

She stared at the three dots.

Sure. But are you grounded or something? Why can't you come to us?

My dad is just being weird, she said. It wasn't untrue but that's about all she could say without sounding like a crazy person and also likely breaching top secret clearances that had no doubt been slapped on top of her traumatic experience.

Okay, see you later, came his reply. Gotta go now.

It wasn't until dark when she got another text from him, letting her know they were on their way.

"Ben!" she called out.

He was in the security room while she was busy watching a stupid number of clip videos of pro-gamers playing one simple yet addicting game at the kitchen table with McDonald next to her.

"Yes?"

"Alfie is coming over for a visit."

"Did you clear it with base security? Your father?"

"Can you? He wants me to meet his boyfriend."

Ben sighed, but she heard tapping on his phone.

Only a second passed before he called back, "We're good, but how about some more warning next time?"

"It just came up!" A few hours ago, but still. It's not like she'd had this planned for days and had failed to let the proper people know.

"I'll be in the room the whole time," Ben added. "Alfie won't think it's weird since he's met me before. McDonald," he said, addressing him, "You can be in the security room."

"Alfie already saw McDonald on campus with me. He knows something is up."

Ben walked in. "Maybe, but his boyfriend doesn't."

Verity couldn't argue with that.

But when Ben opened the door to Alfie and his boyfriend, they were both proven wrong.

Because it turns out she already knew her friend's boyfriend.

Zeph.

"Hey, Ver. Captain hottie," Alfie greeted them.

Ben didn't respond to the nickname but she hid her laugh in a cough. She doubted Zeph wanted to hear his boyfriend talking about another man's attractiveness right in front of him.

But she couldn't exactly blame her friend. Ben *was* handsome.

"Come in," she said to them, leading them into the living room.

She let the two of them take the couch while she took an arm chair and Ben stayed standing in the doorway.

"So, how did you meet?"

They both shared a look, which was more than enough to tell her it was through a dating app that probably put more emphasis on hooking up than actual dating.

The rest of the conversation wasn't particularly special, mostly them just talking about how they stayed up late most nights chatting, or even just hearing each other's breathing as they slept in their respective bedrooms.

She had *awww*'d at how cute it was, earning her an embarrassed glance from Alfie and a very satisfied one from Zeph.

She never would have guessed Joseph was gay but that just went to show that you could never judge a book by its cover. Then again, she didn't really care what the sexual orientation of her friends were. As long as people were in love, happy, and safe in their relationships, who was she to judge?

But what was more surprising was how coincidental it was that he was dating her friend. He hadn't given any indication during this visit that he already knew her to Alfie. But she couldn't exactly expect Joseph to say that he knew her since they were both kidnapped together in space.

It was probably recent events that was making her think about it a little too much. Coincidences happened every day, despite one of her favorite TV character's regular and absolute insistence that they didn't exist.

How many times had she heard her classmates from New York talk about how, despite living in a city of more than eight million souls, they often ran into the same people on the street?

And that was apart from set circumstances that would regularly expose them to a specific cohort? The world was a lot smaller than people thought.

And it would probably get a lot smaller once humanity banded together to fight the impending alien threat. But who knew when that would be?

And that uncertainty was driving her nuts.

12

KNOX

KNOX WATCHED the five men rotating around the otherwise unassuming building on the far end of the base. If a human prisoner being kept there had ever managed to escape their confines, they'd have almost no chance of escaping the base all together before being taken down by any number of the personnel trained to take down such threats and worse.

Worse, of course, meaning him and his kind. Trohm would've been able to escape easily but he was clearly biding his time, waiting for his visit and next set of orders on how to proceed.

Having five guards instead of four made sure was always an extra pair of eyes, should any of the other four be compromised. And the fifth person could step into their place quickly while another was added to the rotation to maintain the level of vigilance.

He'd have to take out four of them without the fifth noticing. Two, would be easy without a question. Three likely wouldn't be a problem though he wasn't a fool enough to say it was an impossibility. Four was the most concerning because it was another opponent to factor in. Fighting all but one of these men could be a small stretch if they put up good fights to last more than a minute each.

There were no guarantee that the fifth wouldn't notice something was amiss while he was fighting the fourth or even third one.

He took a deep breath, centering himself and clearing his mind of the possible negative outcomes. He didn't want to become a self-fulfilling prophecy.

He double-checked his camouflage setting and targeted the most vulnerable guard, the one on the far-side of the building. Even in the worst-case scenario of his suit failing and revealing his presence, the cameras would only see him as a dark blur.

The man barely had time to open his mouth before Knox struck at the guard's vocal chords, silencing him.

Knox used the same hand to grip the connection between the man's neck and shoulder, pinching the pressure point until the man crumpled before him. He could've easily snapped his neck or beheaded him as he'd been framed for doing, but Knox instead held his hand over the man's nose and released a puff of sleeping gas out of his armor's glove for extra insurance that the human would not regain consciousness too soon.

The man's head drooped to the side, and Knox left him there.

He moved onto the next, and repeated the process three times more until he only had one more guard he needed to silence: the fifth and final one.

The man was on higher alert than the others, likely because he couldn't hear his companions anymore, but as Knox was still invisible to the human eye, it was still relatively easy to subdue him. The man wasn't as good at guessing his location as Verity's guard had been, which made him wonder if the humans had been doing extra experimenting at very subtle levels that even their scan had missed.

Which only added another level of tragedy to the young man's gruesome death. He would've made a good subject alongside Verity and the human Captain.

Knox approached the door and activated the unlocking mechanism in his suit. He held his hand to the keypad and saw which ones were pressed most recently based on heat signatures, allowing him to reverse-engineer the code.

He heard the lock disengage and entered without a problem.

There was no extra security sensors or checkpoints inside the building, so he was free to walk down the corridor to the door labeled stairs.

For such a secret base, some of their security seemed unsophisticated. Perhaps they assumed that if anyone was on the base already, they would be vetted enough that they wouldn't be trying to break in anywhere.

Then again, Trohm had told him before about certain places requiring iris scanners and others with security cards which made him wonder if the humans scaled the security measures to what was contained within each structure.

By that logic, he would expect that this building be of a much higher security level but perhaps they were also using reverse psychology. If a jailbreak ever were attempted by external forces, they wouldn't bother to check such an unassuming building to for high-level prisoners.

But humans did not have the same quality tracking beacons Eochronians did. Knox pulled up Trohm's signal again and zoomed down the steps to the basement, and found his agent sitting patiently on the other side of a thick glass wall. His ankles and wrists were bound to the metal chair with chains. Titanium, perhaps, though they looked incredibly fragile in comparison to Eochronian metal.

Knox could see a metal door at the back, allowing humans to enter the cell without needing to remove and reinstall the glass wall.

It would be easy for him to shatter the wall with sound waves at the proper frequency but he had no intention of releasing his spy just yet.

The humans assumed Trohm was alone and couldn't contact anyone else now that he was isolated but they were wrong.

Trohm *could* have contacted him before now, but by waiting he'd let the humans assume that their security measures were working.

Human error: an Eochronian's best friend.

Knox activated the sound wave feature on his suit so if there were any listening devices planted, they would only hear silence. Not even static, which would be a tell-tale sign that something was being hidden.

"How are you?" he asked, speaking their native language.

"Fine, Your Majesty."

"Have they mistreated you?"

His agent smiled. "They've certainly tried. The only real punishment I've been experiencing is this isolation."

"Lonely?"

"Bored, more than anything."

"What have they asked you?" He knew better than to ask what Trohm had told them. His agent would never betray their kind to humans, even if he were in danger of truly being tortured in a way that could harm an Eochronian.

"The usual. My real name, what I am, what my mission is."

How unoriginal. Granted, the ones Aerue, Eiz'm, and the others were administering weren't much more unique aside from Verity being a special case. His interrogators had been looking for information about her father. If he had personally been questioning her, his queries would have certainly taken a more intimate turn since he wanted to learn everything about her.

Of course, they hadn't needed to ask for a lot of personal information because every single human who had been taken was under surveillance for years.

"What do you need me to do, Your Majesty?"

"I'm afraid you'll have to be bored for a little longer as I need you here, gathering more information in case they let anything slip."

Trohm nodded. "Humans are incredibly proud. They think I'm no longer a threat."

Knox smiled. "But we both know better."

He had picked Trohm for this short-term—at least in human terms—undercover assignment on Earth knowing that it wouldn't utilize his agent's impressive fighting abilities, though his recent persona of being part of this special combative space team must have been a welcome change of pace.

"You can check in with me every few days, if you need to. But I want to know things as fast as possible."

"Yes, Your Majesty. Is there anything I should specifically be listening for? I can't fish, unfortunately, or they'll get suspicious. They suffer from hubris but none of the people on this base are all brains and no brawn."

"Nothing specific. Give me everything you can."

"How has your time on Earth been?"

"Entertaining. Zeph took me to a gentleman's club yesterday." Though his other agent's human persona was a rather geeky one, he was in truth a very sexual being who enjoyed his pleasures.

Trohm grinned knowingly. "How was it?"

"Interesting."

"But I have a feeling your mind is too preoccupied to fully appreciate it."

Knox nodded in acknowledgement. "Has she been in to see you?"

"She's not allowed in here. Though, I'm sure she won't let that stop her."

"When she inevitably sneaks in, please do everything you can to learn how she's doing." He turned and started walking away, but not before attaching an invisible listening device to the glass.

"And who?"

Knox stilled. "What?" He was fully aware of the colloquialism that "doing someone" meant having sexual relations, and the idea of Verity having someone other than him—Captain Tenner or even a faceless stranger—made him want to do something reckless, like surprise her in her home so they could finally have another face-to-face talk.

"That was a joke, Your Majesty. I apologize. I've never known her to associate with anyone."

"You'll find out."

"Yes, Your Majesty."

13

VERITY

VERITY TOOK A DEEP BREATH, and focused on pushing all her weight into the ground. The small, loose asphalt pieces still hurt her knee, but she almost appreciated it this time around. It kept her in the here and now, one of the most important things Dr. Hudson had told her when she texted her after their last session, asking her what she could do to prevent another freakout during her next mandatory fight class.

Apparently, her accidental maiming of the cadre wasn't enough for her father to be convinced that she could defend herself better now than before her abduction.

From the last report she'd gotten out of Ben, Wells was expected to be back on base by the end of the month but she doubted he'd be resuming his fight teaching that soon. Maybe she'd send him a gift basket to apologize. She would offer to be his personal assistant to boss around until he was fully healed but with two bodyguards of her own, she doubted it was a possibility.

This time, she was paired up with another STF. Clearly, the higher ups weren't going to risk with her injuring another instructor. She had to wonder if the decision had come from her father or if they had done it without asking for his opinion.

Her sparring partner kept eyeing her like she was going to kill him if he made one false move. But he was wrong. She could accidentally kill him if *she* made one false move, not the other way around.

She'd have to be super careful this time, which meant she had to focus not only on doing the fighting techniques properly and well but also not using her full strength in the execution, lest she accidentally execute one of her father's men.

Her partner went to grab her but she moved faster and grabbed him around the middle, tackling him until they both fell down with him flat on his back. Normally, she would've launched forward like a sprinter at the start of a race but instead, she merely leaned forward as if she were lunging forward, while keeping her upper body low and parallel to the ground.

It was a lot less force, and based on his singular grunt, she hadn't seriously injured him.

He grabbed her wrists and flipped them so he was on top.

Gravity wasn't as mean to her as it had been to him but the move still hurt. She held in the gasp that would reveal just how affected she was. It didn't help that he was still laying on top of her longer than necessary. One hundred and eighty pounds of STF on top of her made it a little hard to breathe.

She hooked his leg with her own and flipped them again before standing up and stepping away from him before he could pull her down again.

He scrambled up and refused to meet her gaze. Maybe he was worried she would tell her father that he copped a feel, despite his hands remaining in completely appropriate places for the close-quarters grappling they were doing.

Her father's lecture and public dressing down of Chapman and Davies was more effective than she thought it would be. Not only had it effectively chastised them—the duo had been avoiding her ever since—it also scared everyone else who might have taken their place as her personal harassers.

They kept going through the exercises demonstrated at the start of the class, switching who played the aggressor after each singular component. Eventually, they started sparring free form without any turns or rules other than fighting safely enough to not seriously or permanently hurt the other.

With every move, she focused on how her muscles felt to keep herself in the current moment and to hold herself back. It accomplished exactly what she hoped it would, and the class finished without any issues.

By the end, she was ready to take a cold shower to clean off the sweat that now covered her body.

Whatever they'd done to her in space had clearly changed the fact that she used to not sweat, and it was a perfect topper to everything else that happened—if only she could turn back the clock.

She met Ben's implacable gaze.

He nodded and he motioned to McDonald.

The three of them departed the rest of the class and she led them back to her home.

On the way there, she texted her father that everything was fine and where they'd be in case he needed any of them.

She had no idea when he'd see it—he'd left early in the morning before she'd even woken up. For what, she didn't know, but it was probably another litany of important meetings.

She unlocked the door, and started walking up the stairs before McDonald blocked her, and went up first.

She rolled her eyes, but hung back until he confirmed the second floor was cleared.

Once he did, she ran into the bathroom and called out, "I'm taking a shower. Don't disturb me unless it's an emergency."

"Yes, ma'am," McDonald said.

Ben didn't answer but she knew he would abide by her order.

Once she was under the spray, she took a deep breath and let the hot water wash away her stress as it beat down on her shoulders, slowly unknotting them.

BY THE TIME Verity went back downstairs to meet her guards, she was starving for lunch. The workout, plus her regularly throwing up probably only served to make her hungrier.

Her hair was still wrapped up in her towel, soaking up the rest of the moisture she hadn't been able to manually squeeze out before leaving the bathroom.

Both of them were seated at the kitchen table, facing the door.

She walked behind them to access the refrigerator and pulled out the ingredients to make a sandwich. Normally, she would do turkey, cheese, lettuce, tomato, and honey mustard but she didn't want to tempt fate by giving her stomach too much to deal with at once.

She also poured a glass of water for herself, and placed it on the counter while she put away the ingredients.

Verity sat down opposite them and finally saw that Ben was frowning down at his phone.

"What's wrong?" she asked.

He held up a finger, and she started eating while she waited for him to be ready.

A few moments passed before he put his phone down and stared at her.

"Have you seen him?"

"Seen who?"

He narrowed his eyes at her, giving her a look that screamed, *don't play dumb*.

She raised an eyebrow in return. She knew he'd understand her retort, *I'm not*.

He continued glaring at her. "Have you snuck him past us?"

Verity wanted to smack herself. How could she have been so slow on the uptake? "Why the hell would I do that?"

"You tell me."

"I wouldn't. Now, tell me what the hell you're going on about."

He turned his phone toward her and she saw a newscaster reporting the from the Vegas strip. The ticker at the bottom of the screen read: *Hospital confirms little girl cured of brain cancer by stranger on the Vegas Strip.*

"You're telling me you had no idea."

"No, I didn't." She had no idea where he was staying, or that he was even still in the area, though she had suspected it, of course. And how would she have ever known that these aliens could cure freaking *cancer*? It's not like she ever got any substantial answers to the questions she'd asked the alien king during their multiple meals together.

"But it's confirmation that he's here."

McDonald cleared his throat. "I don't mean to interrupt but who is the *he* we're talking about?"

"Knox," she answered.

"The alien king."

She stifled a smile. Ben's insistence on using his title instead of his name was perhaps the pettiest thing she'd ever seen him do.

Verity wasn't sure how specific her father had gotten about who they were protecting her from. His name and him being the king might have been excluded.

"He's the one who left a love note to her before we got back."

She was tempted to kick him under the table but there was a chance she might accidentally hit McDonald. If that happened, it would render the whole action pointless since it would alert her other guard that she was secretly trying to shut Ben up.

McDonald's gaze jumped between the two of them, likely sensing his much Ben hated Knox, but he wisely didn't comment on it.

She went back to eating and stopped listening to him. Once

113

she was done, she put her dish in the washer and refilled her glass of water.

"Do either of you want something?"

They both shook their heads.

"Okay. I'll be right back."

Before they could stop her, she ran upstairs again and hung up her towel in the bathroom before grabbing her brush and running it through her hair. She winced when it caught on a particularly large and stubborn knot.

She kept working on it, until it released.

The bathroom door started to open. She grabbed the hairdryer from the cabinet and held it out in front of her. Obviously, she couldn't shoot anyone with it, but it was heavy enough that if she could land a hit in the right spot, it would incapacitate or maybe even kill the intruder.

It opened all the way, revealing McDonald. He held his hands up when he saw her.

She put down her makeshift weapon. "Are you trying to give me a heart attack?"

"No! Sorry."

She sighed and put her things away. "What did you need?"

"To use the…"

She inched past him. "I'll get out of your way."

When she got downstairs and found Ben, standing near the stairway, watching the door.

"Next time he has to go to the head," she said, "Tell him to *knock*."

He nodded.

"What are you watching for?"

He didn't say a word, which was answer enough.

She felt heat prickling at the base of her neck. "Are you mad at me?"

"No."

"Then what's the matter."

"He's still out there. And you're not taking the threat seriously."

"I thought you just said you weren't mad at me."

"I'm not. Frustrated, yes. Mad, no."

"Oh, well, that's so much better."

"This is serious, Verity."

"Ben, I don't need another father. In case you haven't noticed, mine is still alive and kicking." Which, she knew she was incredibly lucky in being able to say. "And don't give me a big brother lecture, either. If I wasn't taking this seriously, I would've tried to ditch my protection detail by now. But I haven't. Because I'm not an idiot."

"Then why do you keep referring to him by his name?"

"That really bugs you, doesn't it?"

He turned his head and gave her a hard look.

She finished walking down the steps and stood in front of him. "I know he's dangerous."

"He's gotten to you."

"He won't again."

"Not what I meant."

Now, it was her turn to glare at him. "I don't know what you're implying, Ben, but you're wrong."

VERITY TOOK another small bite of the mashed potatoes her father had picked up at the dining facility on the way back from his meetings. He'd been gone all day which meant she'd been bored out of her mind after fighting class since he had yet to make good on his promise of buying her a barre so she could keep up with her ballet.

To be fair, though, she probably should've done more stretching and some of the floor exercises.

It would've been better than trying and failing to engage her guards in any types of games.

If she had more than just two, maybe she could've asked at least one to actually spend time with her but she couldn't with such a low number. They both needed to be alert and constantly on the lookout for threats and she wasn't going to push them into losing focus, and therefore taking the brunt of one of her father's tirades.

She loved her father, but when he lost his temper, it wasn't pretty. It was only shouting but still something she tried to avoid. It had never been too much of an issue before now, though her arguing to go to UNLV had been a struggle, even before she'd ever been abducted.

Ben and McDonald had made themselves scarce since he came back, which left her and her father alone in the kitchen, having dinner.

He sat across from her and was eating slower than usual, keeping her snail-like pace. Watching her closely as she took every bite.

You'd think she had a problem with eating based on how intently he was scrutinizing her.

Normally, her speed was much faster but slow and steady seemed to be the only way she could keep food down. It's why she'd only thrown up thrice so far today instead of the five trips to the bathroom that she'd taken the day before by the same time.

Her father paused his progress. "How are you feeling today?"

"Better." Though, as she said the words, she had the sudden urge to vomit again.

She shot up from her seat and ran to the bathroom.

He followed her, and handed her a glass of water once she was done.

She silently toasted him and took a grateful sip.

"How many times today?"

"Four," which meant she was now only one behind yesterday's tally.

"Perhaps you should see Dr. Lane again."

She felt another urge and hunched back over the toilet. When she was done, she brushed her teeth and drank more water. She turned to face her father and nodded.

Verity wanted answers, and Dr. Lane would be able to tell her what was physically wrong with her. Or, at the very least, hopefully let her know that she wasn't pregnant with some type of alien hybrid. She highly doubted it would be a gruesome, fatal birth like the famous scene but she still didn't want an extraterrestrial parasite growing inside her.

"I'll make an appointment for tomorrow," he said.

"It's after hours."

Her father didn't address her as he pulled out his phone and fired off a message.

Dr. Lane would likely answer despite the time of day because it was her father. On this base, his orders were basically the same as a summons from God. No one kept him waiting unless there was an emergency that made it absolutely necessary.

"You have it first thing in the morning. I'll go with you."

Great. That meant a five a.m. wakeup. She wasn't looking forward to that.

"I can go by myself—with Tenner and McDonald, of course," she added.

"No. I'll accompany you."

She'd never really thought about it but her dad always accompanying her to her appointments even after she became a legal adult was a little strange. Then again, he probably wanted to know if there was anything the aliens had done to her.

But she couldn't squash the suspicion that he was keeping secrets from her.

14

KNOX

KNOX STARED at the image on the screen of the black box sitting in the living room. A TV, which was a rather simple example of entertainment technology even by human standards. The images were flat and prone to having bars of incorrect color, breaking up the viewing experience.

How they hadn't fixed those problems while also making strides in the fields of virtual and augmented reality was a mystery to him.

The inequality throughout the world between different cultures was bad enough but for them to not push their technological advances until every aspect of life was optimized was a true shame and waste of potential.

The woman speaking with the microphone said, "And now, we have a story about a girl who was miraculously cured of cancer by a stranger. It was recently verified by the hospital where she was getting ready to start her first round of chemotherapy. I have the father with me right now."

Knox watched as the man who had rightfully been protective of his daughter the day before filled the screen and had the microphone thrust in his face as he was asked questions.

When asked to describe the stranger, Knox leaned forward, curious as to what he would say.

The adjectives were tall, male, lean, and classically handsome.

Knox smiled. They were all complimentary descriptors and he would have loved to know if Verity could truthfully disagree with them. They were also thankfully nonspecific enough that it would be difficult for anyone to find him based off it alone.

Though, the news story had returned to the female reporter who was now asking viewers to send in any information they knew about the mysterious stranger so that he could be properly thanked and also perhaps called upon for additional miracles.

Which brought up a tactic Knox hadn't particularly considered before on a larger scale. But by positioning himself as a savior much as humanity had historically seen his kind, in addition to the people who had witnessed his healing the little girl yesterday, would be a smart way to ingratiate themselves with humans to the point of perhaps being welcomed with open arms rather than a battalion of soldiers and vast collection of weapons, weak as they may be.

Had the capture of the human subjects gone off without discovery, this could have been the way they introduced themselves to humanity. Perhaps, it wasn't too late, given Verity's father's air base hadn't exactly gone public with the information they knew. The large majority of humans had no idea there was any threat—already present or even just looming.

Public opinions sometimes mattered more than facts with humans so it wasn't an impossible course of action.

Perhaps he should contact some of his other moles across the globe and farther away from the air base and tell them to start enacting "miracles."

He shut off the device and returned to his room to continue absorbing the sun's heat. It was a necessary activity for Eochronian survival but it was also an enjoyable one. Being bathed with light and warmth was a very peaceful feeling, and one he couldn't wait to share with his kind once they were all off the mothership and on this planet as their new permanent home.

KNOX COULDN'T HELP the pang of panic that ran through him when he saw Arfilmea was trying to contact him.

Had she somehow found out that he had gone to the human gentleman's club? The only ones who could have told her were Trohm and Zeph but there was no reason for them to betray his confidence to her.

He took a deep breath and answered, bracing himself for whatever she had in store for him.

The projection of her showed her sitting forward, eager to talk to him. "There you are!"

She acted as if she had been trying to contact him for a while and he'd been avoiding her. When, in truth, she hadn't made any effort to talk to him since he arrived before now. Why she was contacting him instead of just badgering her brother for information was a mystery, too.

He sighed and leaned back, putting more distance between them. "What do you need, Arfilmea?"

"You. Back here. Now."

Each word was an auditory punch, and Knox fought the urge to wince. Showing any sign of weakness was unacceptable, especially to her. He was certain she would pounce on it and use it to her own advantage.

He kept his voice even, forcing himself to sound almost bored. "What's wrong?"

She pointed accusingly at him, making him grateful there were five trillion human miles between them.

"As if you don't already know!"

He waited for her to continue. Knowing her, it could be any number of imagined slights against her. Many humans had the sexist belief that females regularly emotionally overreacted but that was actually more of a product of human *males* being hypo-critical in doing exactly that. But regardless of which human sex was more likely to become overly emotional, Arfilmea blew it out of the water, dwarfing their reactions with the magnitude of her own.

"Eiz'm is wreaking havoc," she bemoaned. "He won't stop bossing me and Aerue around and acting like he's the king."

"I know."

"You *know*?"

Maybe Aerue hadn't informed his sister of their conversa-tions, after all.

"Then why aren't you back already?" she demanded.

"Because I'm not done with my work here."

She glared at him. "Don't lie to me. We both know why you're really prolonging your stay. But if you don't return soon, you might not be king anymore. And then where will I be?"

Knox suppressed the urge to roll his eyes. Of course, it was about her. Not the fact that the coup was illegal and Eiz'm would lead their limited numbers to unnecessary war. His rival would likely run their kind into the ground, killing off any chance of their survival at the expense of his own power trip.

"You could always marry him instead," he shot back.

She made a disgusted face. "I can't believe you would even suggest that!"

"You should know me better than to think I'd ever be serious in such an outlandish proposal." Though, it would get her off his back. But he wasn't willing to yield to Eiz'm in any way, including his fiancée, trying as she might be sometimes.

And if Eiz'm and Arfilmea ever were to unite, his life would be a living hell. In such a scenario, he couldn't even count on Aerue to take his side since his sister would be queen.

He sighed. "I'll return soon. I promise."

"I suppose that's the best I'll get from you?"

He nodded.

"Fine. Just know that the longer you're gone, the more unbearable he'll be when you return."

In lieu of an answer, he closed the communication. He'd certainly get a lecture for that once he returned to his ship but, at the moment, he didn't care.

"I WAS WONDERING when I'd be seeing you."

"It has been overdue," a male voice answered.

Not Verity, then.

Knox readjusted his position to get more sunlight and turned the volume up on his listening device so he could hear Trohm's visitor better.

He heard a soft scraping noise. A chair, maybe?

"So, you've been spying on us for years." It wasn't a question.

Trohm remained silent.

"You're not going to defend yourself?"

Again, Knox couldn't hear anything so he assumed Trohm was nonverbally answering. Probably shaking his head.

"How do you contact your king?"

"Do you honestly think I'm going to answer any of your questions? We've had the same training on resisting interrogation techniques."

"And more, I'll bet."

It was an accurate assumption but didn't begin to cover how much experience Trohm had. He doubted the human was even considering the millions of years of combat and the few hundred more for espionage training.

Knox heard Trohm chuckle.

"You could say that," his agent answered.

There was a sigh and Knox wasn't entirely sure whether it came from either Trohm or the Captain.

He was sure they were both annoyed with each other though

Trohm was likely more bothered by the uncomfortable seat than the human was by the lack of answers.

"Okay," the Captain started again. "If you won't talk, then you can just listen."

"Listen to what?"

"Do you want me to gag you? Because I will."

"Well, we both know I was never super good at keeping my mouth shut."

"Unless it was keeping this giant secret of the fact that you're not even human. But you've already established you're not going to talk about that."

"Correct."

"So, just so we're clear, when we first met, you already knew all about the true workings of the base?"

There wasn't a verbal response but Knox knew the answer was yes. Even though Trohm specifically hadn't been planted within any of the country's military branches before he became Tristan, he'd had moles in every branch of every country's military throughout time.

He had a better understanding of human history than most humans, who were often only taught a limited number of perspectives on past events to the point that they were unable to fully consider and anticipate other nation's actions.

"And you very quickly became friends with me, but that was because how close I am to General Landau, wasn't it? Getting close to Verity must have only made your job that much easier."

"Well, hanging out with her certainly wasn't a hardship. She's certainly a lot more fun than your stuffy ass. You really should learn to let loose more. At least she balanced you out."

"And you constantly tried to corrupt her. At least I was there to protect her from your undue influence. And do you honestly think I'm going to take any advice from you now that I know you're a traitor? I'm certainly not going to let my guard down now."

"Now that you're guarding her?"

"Who told you that?"

"Come on, Tenner. You know everyone is talking about the two of you since got back. People hearing you're now staying under the same roof as her? People are obviously going to speculate. I even heard someone started a pool on whether you'll have the guts to sleep with her."

There were some footsteps followed by a loud smack. No doubt, the human had lost his temper and slapped Knox's agent. Of course, it would barely sting one of his kind given how weak a human's maximum strength was compared to that of an Eochronian.

Trohm said, "I wouldn't mention the pool to the General. He might kill you. And if you rat out whoever started the pool—assuming you can get someone to rat them out—you'll cost a lot of people a lot of money. And then you'll have enemies on base, too."

"So, your king isn't on base yet?"

"Well, he already was, right? Would you really be surprised that he accomplished it again?"

Knox heard footsteps again, getting closer to the listening device on the glass. Then came the slight shifting of the chair, a noise that would be too quiet for a human to hear. If he had to guess, the human had seated himself again farther away from Trohm. Perhaps he needed the distance to deny himself the temptation of hitting Trohm again.

"Answer the question."

"I thought you just wanted me to listen."

"If you're an alien, then how have you pretended to be human this whole time? Clearly your kind is stronger than us—" the human didn't seem happy admitting that.

"I bet that was was hard for you to say, wasn't it?"

"I'm mature enough that I can acknowledge the strength of my enemies."

"I'm an enemy now?"

"You've always been an enemy. We just didn't know it."

"It's not like I ever hurt any of you."

"You let in your asshole friends who proceeded to kidnap and torture us. I'd say that was harmful to us. So, don't pretend you've only been benign in your deception. What I don't understand is how you never got discovered during the annual physicals unless... there's another one of you who's a medic."

Knox had to admit the man was intelligent. Though, it wasn't a surprise. It was clear Verity didn't suffer fools and he was positive that was a trait she learned from her father, who obviously liked and trusted the captain enough to guard his only daughter.

Trohm yawned and Knox couldn't help the chuckle that escaped. The listening device was one-way so there was no danger of them hearing him.

There was little chance that his agent was genuinely tired because while he was being kept in a basement without any sunlight, it took more than a few human days for the effects to noticeably deplete.

His repeated sunbathing since arriving on Earth was a decadent indulgence he hadn't been able to enjoy since they were forced to evacuate their home planet. The energy he was absorbing would keep him going for about a human month before he'd need more.

While they were all aboard his ship, Trohm had regularly used the heat atrium and would be good for at least a week, if not longer since he wasn't using up the energy while being detained.

"Am I boring you?" the human captain snapped. "Because if you'd like something more exciting, I'm sure I can arrange that for you."

"It wasn't all a lie, you know. I really did consider you and Verity a friend. Kind of like your *Three Musketeers*."

"No, I don't. And it doesn't matter. Besides, you've been in this country long enough to know that story didn't originate here so it's not *my* anything."

"But I considered you a brother, not just a friend." He sounded both sad and pissed off in equal measure. "And you stabbed me in the back."

"If I had done that literally, you'd be in a wheelchair if not in the ground."

"If I were in your position, you'd already be six feet under. That would be the only option. I don't believe in letting enemies live long enough to return the favor."

"So, you're here to execute me?" Trohm sounded rather disappointed the prospect.

It would be impossible, of course, but apparently his agent didn't like the idea of being ordered dead. Not that he could blame him. No one was ever excited by considering their eventual demise.

"No," the human answered. "They think you're better off alive and no one will listen to me when I tell them that you won't talk."

"See? You do know me well."

Knox heard footsteps again, moving further away. "Not well enough, obviously. I hope you enjoyed your life, however long it really was." The last words were dripping with skepticism. "Because the moment they realize I am right, you'll be executed and none of us will shed any tears."

"Aw, don't say that. At least let me fantasize that someone will mourn me at my funeral."

"You think the military is going to pay for the funeral of a traitor? You're going to be buried where no one will ever find you. Assuming they don't decide to dissect you instead. Hell, they might even start while you're still alive."

"I assume you'd think that would be an appropriate example of *quid pro quo* but if you remember correctly, no one actually dissected you, so you'd be going a bit overboard."

"Really? And here I thought you'd be getting off easy."

"You're enjoying this, aren't you? I never pegged you for having a sadistic side."

Knox could hear the smile in his agent's voice even before he added another verbal barb.

"Even I can be wrong, sometimes."

"Something we have in common. But I'm not going to be paying for my mistake with my life."

"Only because we never planned to kill you."

Knox sat up. What was he doing?

"So, what was your plan? Or, I suppose I should say *is* because your kind doesn't seem the kind to be deterred from one mishap. And it's not like we were able to rescue all of the humans you kidnapped so there's a very good chance you are already moving ahead since we don't know enough to actively interfere."

"Well, I'm going to disappoint you because I'm not about to help you fill in the gaps."

"You're wrong. You'd be disappointing me if you did. I'd lose any respect I ever had for you."

"I thought you hated me?"

"Those emotions are not mutually exclusive, jackass."

Knox heard the chair move again, the beeping of a code being entered, and then the sound a door opening.

"We're done here," the human captain said.

"Say hi to Verity for me."

"Go to hell."

15

VERITY

VERITY STARED at the ceiling and tracked the base's security lights dancing across the white surface. Though her shades were closed, she always had them tilted up so that if someone was crazy enough to have a death wish by trying to spy into her room, they wouldn't be able to see much.

And whenever she napped on the weekends, it was better than having sunlight streaming down onto her in her bed. At night, however, it was the opposite of helpful because she often stared at the light instead of the back of her eyelids. She should start adjusting her blinds before nightfall but every time she told herself she would, she would forget at the next opportunity. It was a pointless cycle that was biting her in the ass right now as she was unable to fall asleep.

As far as she knew, her father was sleeping in his room down the hall and one of her guards likely was, too, though she didn't know who was taking the early shift tonight. If she was lucky, it was Ben. He'd left her with McDonald and another STF in the afternoon when she was busy doing dance exercises with the newly arrived barre.

Her dad had kept his word after all.

She had no idea if Ben had cleared his absence with her father but she wasn't about to ask her dad and potentially get him in trouble. She had the sneaking suspicion he had headed to where they were keeping Trohm because he had refused to answer her questions about his destination, even when she'd pressed him.

If she hadn't had four eyes on her at the time, she would've tried to follow him but if she had to guess, it was on the other side of the base where she barely saw personnel. It was the most secret place on their already secret corner of the world, even with all the conspiracy theories that circulated around the internet. Those crazy conjectures, in fact, were a smoke screen on their own in addition to the military's other top secret measures. She wouldn't even put it past her father to have some of the cyber dogs fanning the flames of the online speculation because ironically, one of the best ways to discredit the conspiracy was to feed into it more because it caused believers to appear even more crazy to nonbelievers. The psychological manipulation there would make Freud proud. She wondered what Dr. Hudson would say about it if she were privy to the details.

Great. Now her mind was spiraling so much that she felt more wired than she did before.

Verity slipped out of her sheets and padded across her room in the dark to grab her phone off the charger. She always kept it there with an alarm set for the morning so she couldn't snooze and fall back asleep after rolling over. She'd made that mistake once when her mother was still alive and she'd gotten stuck with extra chores courtesy of her father even though her mother had tried to advocate for her based on the fact that she was a growing girl who needed sleep to develop properly. It hadn't worked on convincing him but her mother had tried her best.

She squinted at the screen. Even though she turned the brightness all the way down, it was still blinding in the context of her dark room. It read *2:27am* which meant she'd been unable to fall asleep for almost three hours already and she wasn't getting any sleepier as time went on.

She forced her eyes to stay open so the sensor could read her face accurately and unlock her phone.

She pulled up Ben's phone number—something he'd given to her when she first went off to college in case of an emergency—and texted him. Are you awake?

Three dots appeared for only a moment before the single word response came through. Yes.

Come up?
Is something wrong?
Can't sleep.
Be right there. I need to wake McDonald up first.

Verity climbed back into bed and turned on her phone's flashlight, aiming it at the floor in front of her door so she could see him when he entered. She could shine it right at the door in case there was an intruder but she would've already been woken up by her father or Ben if that were the case. And since that hadn't happened, shining her light at eye level would only be cruel to him.

She heard the hushed voices of Ben and McDonald, no doubt explaining the situation and telling him to keep his mouth shut about it. They stopped and a few seconds passed before his footsteps quietly moved up the stairs.

She'd always been able to hear things that should otherwise be silent. And that ability had only become more prominent since she came back home. It was one of the reasons she couldn't seem to fall asleep but it didn't explain why she was having nightmares even when she was lucky enough to be dreaming.

According to Dr. Hudson, those were courtesy of the stress she experienced and was still experiencing because of what happened to her.

Knowing the reason was great and all but it didn't exactly help her in fighting the effects of the cause even though that's what the psychiatrist insisted therapy would do for her. If only she could fast-forward to that part of the psychological healing process.

The door opened and she saw Ben's silhouette fill the frame.

She didn't say anything as he padded across her carpet and closed the door.

"If your father catches me in here, I'm dead, you know that, right?"

"I promise to give a very nice eulogy at your funeral."

"It's not funny, Verity." He sat down in her desk chair on the opposite side of her room.

"If you're going to sit all the way over there, I can't whisper as well. And then if my dad hears…"

He moved to the edge of her bed, perching on it. "This was your plan all along, wasn't it? To get me into bed with you?"

Verity felt her cheeks burning and was glad the lights were off so he couldn't see her reaction. Maybe he *did* know about her crush.

"Technically, you're *on* my bed."

He didn't verbally answer but she could see him smile despite their sitting in the dark.

"So, you can't sleep?"

She shook her head. "What about you?"

"I was already up."

She lightly kicked him through her blanket, making contact with his hard thigh. "You know what I mean."

"Same."

"Then how are you handling it? Especially now that you're… watching me."

"Lots of caffeine."

"Well, that's definitely not helping you get any sleep."

"Better awake than dead."

"I'm not going to die if you fall asleep during your watch."

"But I will."

"If you're talking about Knox, I don't think he would—"

"Believe me, he'd love to. But whether it's at his hands or your father's because I dropped the ball, I'd be dead. So, like I said, awake is better than dead."

She frowned but didn't have anything to say to that other than what she already had. But she didn't want the conversation to end just yet, either.

"Maybe I should take a page out of your book, then," she finally replied.

He shook his head. "Probably not a good idea. I'd hate for you to be too jumpy to focus throughout the day."

"Focus on what? It's not like I'm going to classes right now." She couldn't help the frustration leaking into her voice. "And it doesn't take a lot of brain power to hold onto a barre and do simple exercises in the living room."

"For you, maybe. I'd be thinking about every move."

"Is that you offering to let me teach you ballet?"

"What specifically in what I just said makes you think that?"

She shrugged. "Just thought I'd ask."

"What was your plan in calling me up here? Talk all night?"

It was a good question. She'd been hoping to pass the time until she was tired enough to fall asleep without any dreams, good or bad. She just wanted a good night's sleep and pure exhaustion was the only way she'd ever been able to accomplish it in the past. Though, she'd never had to deal with nightmares once she was old enough to grow out of them. She had a brief relapse after her mother died, where her brain mixed the plots of some stories she'd read with her mom being murdered by the evil villains, even though her mom had died of natural causes. It was just the dream trauma of losing her mother again over and over for a few months until school had ramped up with more intense homework every day of the week.

High school and college only added more to her daily plate but she'd long grown accustomed to the physically grueling schedule, so much so that it took an especially long and demanding day to yield a dreamless night.

But talking to Ben wasn't doing anything to lull her asleep. She was still exhausted, in an existential way, but she was also waking up in other ways now that he was alone with her in her room. At night. In the dark.

If he had any idea of where her mind had gone, he didn't show it by moving away or freezing like an animal suddenly realizing it was about to be eaten. "Hello? Earth to Verity?" he finally prompted her after her silence dragged out too long.

"Sorry. I zoned out."

"Enough to fall asleep?"

She shrugged. "Maybe?"

"Want me to leave?"

"No."

He hissed out a breath, though she couldn't tell if it was from frustration with her request or something else like having to resist her. It was probably just wishful thinking on her part but a girl could hope.

"Then what do you want me to do?"

"Stay here with me?" Sleep probably was addling his judgment because there was no way she would have ever been this forward with him otherwise. But she couldn't bring herself to take back the request.

"And if your father catches me here?"

"We'll tell him the truth."

"Which is?"

"I couldn't sleep so I asked to chat with you and you stayed here to watch over me."

He snorted but didn't have a comeback.

She smiled in victory.

She moved out from under her blankets and sat next to him, pressing her thigh to his.

"Verity…" his voice was a low warning.

She turned toward him and spoke eye level with his neck. If she leaned forward, she could kiss his jawline but she wasn't going to cross that line without some consent and encouragement. "You've never wondered?"

He turned his head, bringing his lips in line with her forehead. "It's not appropriate."

"That's not a yes or no answer."

He sighed, the puff of breath ruffling her hairline a little.

"Yes," he said. "But it can't happen."

"Why not? No one will know."

"The whole base will find out."

"Only if you tell them."

"Or McDonald."

"You're his superior. You can order him to keep it to himself."

"There's a pool going on whether we do. There's more on us than not." His tone was slightly accusatory.

"Why are you saying it like that? It's not as if I started it. Though, honestly, if they're going to bet on us, I think *we* should be getting the cash. So?"

If he was trying to reject her, she needed to hear it in no uncertain terms so she could put the nail in the coffin of her crush and maybe finally move on. Otherwise, she'd continue wondering the same way she had already been doing for years.

"Verity, you're putting me in a difficult position."

She leaned back, giving him the space he was nonverbally asking for.

"You're right. I'm sorry."

His next move caught her off guard.

Before she knew it, he was cradling the back of her head with one hand while the other wrapped around her lower back and pulled her close as his lips closed over hers in a kiss.

Her mouth opened to let him inside and she kissed him back. But even as her longtime dream was coming true, she had the awful confirmation that it was no longer what she wanted. It's not that the kiss was bad—hell, it wasn't even over yet—but it wasn't all-consuming and it didn't light up her body like someone else's had, which was enough to pour cold water over the situation, dousing any remaining flame she might have been able to save for Ben.

Verity heard a noise, almost like a violent gust of wind even though it was a still summer night. She jerked back as if burned. She glanced at her door but it was closed. She turned to her window and saw a shimmer of movement the same way she had the night she was abducted.

"You okay?" Ben asked, drawing her attention back to him.

She forced a smile. "Yeah. I just thought I saw something out there."

He stepped up beside her and looked into the darkness. "I don't see anything."

She couldn't anymore. Whatever had been out there was gone.

Verity sat back down on her bed.

Ben stayed standing. "So... what do you think?"

"If you have to ask, isn't that a bad sign? But... I get what you mean."

His shoulders dropped in relief. "I'm glad it wasn't just me."

"We're still friends, right?"

"Of course. "Do you have another blanket somewhere?"

She nodded. "Top shelf."

He silently slid open the closet door and grabbed the blanket and a spare pillow that sat on top of it.

She heard him make a bed on the floor and him sit back in the chair as he pulled out his phone and texted McDonald downstairs, no doubt to let him know of the updated situation.

"Are you going to sleep now?"

"Not my time yet."

She sighed and lay back down, tucking herself under the covers again but kicking one leg over the side of the blankets. She'd never been like those memes that were afraid to have a foot out in case monsters under the bed came to drag her to hell. She always had to or she inevitably overheated in her sleep. And there was no way she wanted to wake up sweaty if Ben was going to stay the night and watch her in her sleep.

But it was nothing like how she felt going to bed every time on the space ship, knowing Knox or his soldiers were watching her like an ant under a magnifying glass.

Despite the disheartening realization that she and Ben weren't a good match in the way she'd been fantasizing about, his presence really did make her feel safer and knowing he would protect her was the exact security she'd been missing ever since this whole mess started.

"Goodnight, Ben," she whispered.

"Goodnight, Verity."

She closed her eyes and waited for sleep to take her, hoping it would come quickly and that Ben would still be there when she woke up.

16

KNOX

KNOX LAY on the roof of the Landau house next to where Verity's window looked out into the night. He was currently blending into the shingles to avoid detection by anyone who might pass by.

His head practically hung off the edge of the roof so he could have a good view of her in bed. Though her shades were arranged to block people from looking in, he was still able to see her thanks to his kind's ability to sense infrared heat. It wasn't exactly night vision as imagined by humans but closer to thermal vision as used by human scientists and some military groups. Verity's body was now appearing cooler than a normal human's but that wasn't surprising given the changes that were happening to her, even if she didn't fully realize it yet. Right now, he could see she was staring at the ceiling. He wondered what was going through her mind.

He could hear one guard milling around downstairs, the deep breathing of the other, and Verity's father sleeping in his room.

Then he saw her move across the room.

Knox shifted his position to sit in front of her window. It was less comfortable than the reclining position but it gave him a full view of her picking her phone off a vertical stand, lighting up the screen.

She turned it too quickly for him to read it, but he heard her start tapping on the screen. The sound was sub-audible for a human but it was there all the same.

Before he could wonder what she was doing, he heard a small ping on a device downstairs. Then he could hear the human captain speaking to the other guard, letting him know he was going upstairs, to stay awake, and to not breathe a word about it to anyone.

Knox felt a point of heat blossom at the base of his head, and an invisible band of tension squeezing a tight ring around his chest. The human captain was about to enter Verity's room while he was stuck outside, watching their interaction and unable to do anything about it.

Verity moved back to her original position under her blankets but he stayed where he was. He didn't want to give up his new, unobstructed view of the whole room.

The door opened and the human entered, slowly closing the door to minimize the sound. Likely to avoid detection by Verity's father.

Knox doubted the General would appreciate learning the human had entered his daughter's room alone at night. He was almost tempted to make a sound loud enough to alert the older man and get the Captain in trouble, but doing so would alert the household of his presence. Because once they started talking and realized none of them had made the noise, they would be on high alert.

He watched her guard sit down at her desk and breathed a short-lived sigh of relief when the man quickly moved to the edge of the bed.

They started talking about how they were adjusting to life back on Earth and then the topic turned to the fear of her father discovering them together.

The human talked about how he was likely going to die because of it at the General's hand or Knox's.

Knox sat up straighter when he heard Verity say his name in an almost defense of him as she stated that he wouldn't kill the human.

Said human argued back that he certainly wanted to murder him.

They were both right. While he definitely would *like* to do so every so often, an urge that grew more pressing every time he saw the man close to Verity, Knox wasn't about to kill off the second-best subject in his project.

Knox listened as they talked more about less important things though he learned that Verity was still dancing at home. He made a mental note to come by during the day to see that but was pulled back into the present when he saw her move to sit next to the Captain.

And then they started talking about why they should or shouldn't give into their feelings for each other. Knox backed up, feeling a knot of equal parts despair and anger forming in his stomach. But that was nothing compared to the gut punch he felt when he saw them actually kiss.

He looked away and jumped off the roof, running back to Zeph's home and leaving them behind though the image of them together was burned into his memory like a brand.

WHEN HE GOT BACK, he heard Zeph and another person in his agent's bedroom. Likely, the boyfriend.

Knox slipped into the guest room and closed the door. He didn't want the human seeing him. The more people who knew where he was, the greater chance of his being discovered, even with his technological safeguards.

No longer needing the capability to be invisible, he changed out of his armor and into a pair of sleeping clothes his agent had insisted on he get. Apparently, it wasn't acceptable to wear a silk suit to bed. Though, the sleeping clothes he received were also silk so he couldn't complain about that, only to question what was the point if they're already so similar.

He shook his head. Humans were confusing. Clothes were clothes but some were allowed publicly, while others weren't. And it wasn't solely about how revealing they were, as proven by the women he'd seen on the sidewalk of the Vegas Strip.

His kind either wore clothes, or they didn't, depending on how they felt and whether they wanted to telegraph style at any moment. The only time clothing was nonnegotiable had been in battle to better protect themselves or at royal events to show respect for the occasion. And he'd insisted on it once they'd brought the humans on board to not frighten them.

But there was nothing in Eochronian culture that dictated some clothes to be only worn behind closed doors.

He started pacing the room, focusing on keeping his footfalls light so as not to alert Zeph's guest that someone else was in the house. Unfortunately, he couldn't walk silently enough to avoid his agent hearing him but hopefully he wasn't being too distracting. Though, he doubted that would be a problem. Zeph was very good at zoning out the world when he was focused on something, and that applied to everything from his work ethic to the attention he gave his lovers.

Knox was similar, but he could get distracted easier if it came as a surprise and it took longer for him to get back into a flow state of complete concentration.

But he didn't want to be concentrating on what was currently in his mind, which was still the memory of Verity kissing her human Captain. And making sure he was quiet wasn't enough of a challenge to fully engage his mind as a good distraction.

Thinking of Verity was always a distraction that was impossible to get around but therein lied the problem. Because now he needed another distraction to move him *away* from her, and he'd never once succeeded on that front before.

But it wasn't as if he didn't have other things he *should* be thinking about. The problem of Eiz'm, for one thing. Arfilmea, though less of a problem than his rival, was another person he needed to consider his next move with. Depending on how those two situations panned out, he might also have to consider Aerue, though he doubted it would come to that.

But he found his mind turning to the adjacent topic of what to do about the Captain. It wasn't thinking about the one human female who drove him mad but it was just skirting the edges, teetering closer to her magnetic pull as his main thoughts about the man were about how to get him away from Verity, not how to recapture him for the project, though those two considerations could be combined to solve each other.

They weren't thoughts totally devoid of her influence, but it was progress, so Knox continued down the mental path, trying to find a way to reacquire the Captain.

Another kidnapping attempt within the base was out. It could work but it wasn't worth the hassle anymore now that the humans were aware of the potential for an attack by them. It wouldn't be nearly as neat as the first time.

If the man had been guarding Verity while she was at school, he potentially could have taken him then but he hadn't been and there was a good chance Knox would have had to fight him, too, potentially alerting her to the altercation before he could get him away from her. It was a pointless thought experiment to engage in, anyway, because Verity was now restricted to base.

And for the time being, the captain was glued to her side— with the exception of when he went to interrogate Trohm, of course.

Knox wondered if she knew what he had done. She was intelligent enough to guess but perhaps she assumed he had been given extra orders. Though he couldn't imagine the General actually doing so, effectively splitting the man's focus between guarding his daughter and something else. He suspected Verity would know that about her father.

If only it were a real possibility, then he could more easily target the man while he was alone. The danger of being discovered on base would be worth it in his eyes, but it would certainly earn him a lecture from Aerue, once his right hand found out about it. By then, of course, it wouldn't matter.

But that was another impossible scenario.

Knox sighed. He kept running into dead ends around the human Captain, yet another way the man was an obstacle in his way.

Perhaps it was time he switched focus, at least for a little while, and allow his brain to work on it in the background while he solved a different problem.

At least with Eiz'm, he didn't need to worry about being discovered by his own kind. The main problem was being away from them, and his throne, though he knew it was more of a prop than anything else. The only times he ever sat in it was during official events or when briefing his soldiers. But symbols could be important, especially those that projected authority and power.

And if Eiz'm were sitting in it while he was gone, there was a good chance that the people who disagreed with him on the project would be swayed to follow his rival in his absence.

And based on what Aerue had reported, it was already happening with frightening efficacy.

He could only imagine the number of his council who had switched sides. Quallokh and Zrelhlm were at the top of his list, given how vocal they were during his last meeting with him. Though neither of them appeared to want to unseat him from the throne, they both clearly didn't approve of his current plans for their kind regarding the experimental program and his postponing of his royal wedding. Though it was kind of sexist for them to not also partially blame his betrothed's part in that decision. Granted, he was the king and if he had wanted to overrule her, he could have, so maybe he should give them the benefit of the doubt on that score.

But he wasn't in a particularly generous mood to do so with individuals he was sure would stab him in the back—figuratively, since they were not the kind to get their hands dirty, they preferred political warfare to the literal kind—the moment he stepped back aboard the mothership. Even in their support of Eiz'm's militaristic campaign, Knox couldn't imagine them fighting alongside the soldiers they would be sending into the fray.

At least when his grandfather was conquering other species and planets, he was leading them into the charge, armed and capable of doing as much damage as his highest-ranking officials.

If he were on a warpath, he'd follow his ancestor's example. Not to make him proud by any means, he didn't owe him anything other than his right to the throne, but because a good leader never put his followers in a risky situation he wasn't willing to enter himself.

Knox had left Aerue in charge but it was clear Eiz'm was already circumventing his second-in-command's ability to rule in his absence, which left him with few options, though he could perhaps contact Dr. Mak'en and weaponize his science teams to engage in espionage on his enemy and report directly to him. It would effectively cut out Aerue from the loop but perhaps doing so would protect his friend. If Eiz'm ever suspected that Aerue were feeding him information that he'd secretly gotten through other means, Knox was certain Eiz'm would torture all the true royalists who sided with him, the rightful king.

He wondered if Quallokh would object to the abuse of their own kind if it weren't a consequence of harming humans but rejecting the coup. If he didn't he would be a hypocrite, but what politician wasn't at some level?

Even Knox couldn't claim to be above it in some ways as Verity's presence had clearly proven.

Arfilmea was probably having the same complaints as Zrelhlm now that she believed he was putting Verity above her, and he couldn't exactly refute her assumption anymore like he could while they were all on his ship together. At least there, he could play at prioritizing his fiancée with their liaisons in addition to his meals with the captivating human female.

But his presence on Earth instead of personally handling the Eiz'm situation spoke to his true emotions more than he was able to verbally articulate to anyone—including himself.

He needed to get his obsession in check but it was similar to the raercaith plant, so beautiful, fragrantly intoxicating, and delightfully tasty to the point that most people didn't realize they were being poisoned by consuming the fruit before it was too late. Knox smiled. Perhaps he'd show Verity one day, though he'd warn her of its danger before hand, and protect her if her willpower failed.

But that was a consideration for the future, and not one he could realistically entertain until his current problems were solved.

He stopped pacing and finally lay down on his bed, staring outside the window into the dark and resigned himself to a restless night.

17

VERITY

VERITY FELT the eyes on her as her father, Ben, and McDonald escorted her into the medical building.

No one said a thing as they showed their badges and rode in the elevator to the floor where 's office was.

The receptionist nodded at them as the doors slid open. "Dr. Lane will be ready in just a moment."

A nurse came out and led Verity into an examination room, leaving the three men behind to wait for her.

She waited while the nurse took her temperature and blood pressure. She'd already been weighed her first day back so she shouldn't have to do it again, but the nurse logged it in the computer on the desk and said, "Please take off your shoes and step onto the scale," as she input the numbers the temperature and cuff displayed.

She shouldn't have been surprised. Her father had texted Dr. Lane about her vomiting when scheduling this impromptu appointment, after all.

Verity did so and waited for the nurse to move the metal slider. She had seen it done enough times that she could have done it herself if moving wouldn't have altered the result. She

didn't have to wait long, and they soon discovered that she had lost about a pound since her last weigh-in, three days ago.

It wasn't a good sign but if she was losing weight, maybe it meant she wasn't pregnant after all. Because wouldn't she be gaining weight instead? She knew some people didn't change weight much while pregnant but she'd never heard of someone weighing *less* while carrying a baby.

The nurse wrote down the number and directed her to hop back up onto the examination table.

Verity did and stared at the clock as her mind began to spin out the possible explanations for the weight loss.

It wasn't an impossible or particularly unhealthy feat for many people, as long as it was done with medical advice and care. But her situation was different. She wasn't trying to lose weight, whether it be for training purposes or even for a stupid fad diet that usually eventually backfired. She had lost the weight merely from throwing up since her diet and water intake hadn't changed from her normal routine before she'd been taken to space.

If she found a way to stop vomiting, would that solve the problem? Or would she continue losing weight until she was skin and bones? The idea was scarier than she wanted to admit.

Verity liked to think she was more accepting than her father that some things didn't have solutions. Medical issues weren't something she was okay with falling into that category, but she had the sinking feeling there wasn't anything else to do but wait out her symptoms and hoped they got better.

She doubted it.

Maybe the aliens had done something to her where she could no longer eat human food? Her stomach muscles hurt from the constant physical act of regurgitation but it didn't feel like a food intolerance based on what she'd heard some friends say about eating gluten or dairy. It would explain why her body kept rejecting it, but then what was she supposed to do? It's not as if she could get alien food on Earth. Even if she could, she wasn't sure she wanted to, since it would likely only continue whatever experiment they'd started on her.

But she didn't want to die, either, and that meant she couldn't let herself waste away.

She took a calming breath. Maybe she was overreacting and it was a normal stress response due to the trauma she experienced. Why hadn't she thought to ask Dr. Hudson that during a past session? She'd do it now but there wasn't any cell service in the medical building.

Then again, wouldn't her therapist have told her that unprompted once she heard of the vomiting? Maybe her not bringing it up was proof enough that it wasn't a psychosomatic reaction.

The door opened, and Dr. Lane entered.

The nurse left and the door closed behind her.

"Hello, Verity. I didn't expect to see you again so soon. How are you?"

"Not great."

"Has the vomiting gotten worse?"

"It hasn't gotten better."

The doctor nodded. "Anything else?"

"I can't sleep." That was something she hadn't told her father, and hadn't yet experienced when she was last here.

"How so?"

"My mind won't shut off." She wasn't about to go into the nightmares with her. She already wasn't a huge fan of going into it with Dr. Hudson but at least a therapist could help with them. What was an internist going to do? Tell her to go to sleep at a different time? As far as she knew, nightmares didn't care about what a clock said.

"Anxiety?"

She nodded.

"Have you talked to your therapist about it?"

She stared at her.

"Your father let me know you were seeing one since your return," the doctor explained, answering her unspoken question.

It wasn't surprising or even inappropriate but why did it feel like an invasion of privacy?

Maybe it was a holdover from having none in space, but having people talk about her therapy behind her back didn't sit well with her. She could already feel a knot of anxiety forming in her stomach. It wasn't that she was ashamed of being in therapy, even though she still wasn't one hundred percent sold on its efficacy. But it was incredibly personal and she would never discuss or speculate on what someone was doing, unless it was a matter of life and death, either the patient's or the potential for the patient to do harm to someone else.

Basically, she wouldn't violate someone's HIPAA rights even though she wasn't a doctor or therapist, and therefore not technically bound by those rules.

"Are you experiencing any other symptoms? Dizziness, fatigue, cramps, spotting?"

Verity knew they were the early signs of pregnancy—her father had probably stated their shared fear about it—and she was glad to say, "Dizziness and fatigue, but the first only happens when I've been in the heat and I'm probably just tired from not sleeping well." But maybe she was wrong and they were all connected. And just because she didn't have *all* the symptoms that didn't mean she definitely wasn't pregnant. Who knew what she could expect if she was pregnant with an alien baby.

"I'd like to take a few blood tests, just to rule out all possibilities."

"Like what?"

"Pregnancy. Some food intolerances which can develop over a person's life time. Anemia, liver and lipid profiles, thyroid, and tuberculosis, too. I don't expect any of these to come back positive, but at least we'll know."

Verity mostly believed her but the doctor's expression when

she said pregnancy belied the fact that the professional likely shared her suspicion, however far-fetched it might be.

"I'll send the nurse in for the draw, and then you will be able to go. I'll contact you once I know the test results, but like I said, I'm sure there's nothing to worry about."

Verity forced a smile, and rolled her sleeve up in anticipation of the needle.

The nurse entered, sanitized the area, and stuck her with the needle, and plugged in one of the tubes to start collecting the blood.

Verity winced as the needle went in—she could always feel it, even when the thinnest ones were used—but she was glad that it was immediately flowing. At least she wouldn't need to be stuck another time.

It was a lot better than past times but it wasn't as painless as the blood draw she'd experienced in space.

Once the first vial was mostly filled, the nurse removed it from the chamber and plugged in another. She repeated the process two more times before she withdrew the needle and placed gauze over the spot before securing a bandaid over it.

Verity watched the woman swirl and shake the vials of her blood, mixing with the different colored gels at the bottom of each one. It was almost like a strange rainbow, though clear and blue were missing—the colors she'd seen so often in space.

She rolled down her sleeve and walked out of the room and back to the waiting room.

Her father, Ben, and McDonald were there as she'd left them, but so was Zeph.

At her appearance, her father and Zeph rose, going to the back area where she'd just come from.

Was he getting tested, too? If so, why not Ben? Unless that's what Ben was doing yesterday when he went off by himself and she was wrong about him sneaking off to talk to Trohm.

She glanced at her guards, and neither of them looked at her as they stood, and called the elevator.

Maybe they didn't know what was happening, but she could hear her father, Zeph, and Dr. Hudson's voices faintly discussing her, despite the distance and multiple doors between them. The word *anomaly* kept resurfacing and it only made the knot in her stomach tighten further. She didn't have to be a brilliant scientist to know that it meant things weren't normal. The questions she had now were *how* and how bad was the situation, and what could she do about it?

VERITY HELD in a frustrated scream when she tipped over for the third time due to a round of dizziness that seemed to rear its ugly head every time she lowered her heart below her extended leg as it reached up to the ceiling.

She lowered her foot and returned to en pointe with both and let go of the barre. When she didn't tip over at all, it was clear that the symptom wasn't universal. But given she'd also felt it when she stretched her leg on the barre, a position that kept her heart clearly above her legs, she also felt it, so it was a real random toss up whether each move was going to make her feel as if she were barreling toward the ground, or wish she was sitting.

McDonald was sitting on their couch, watching her, though she doubted he was aware of her internal struggle as his gaze hadn't strayed from her legs since Ben had gone into the security room to monitor the security cameras.

She could remind him that her eyes were in her head, but she didn't really care if he was ogling her. It's not like he was harassing her, and she wasn't into him. She doubted he was into her beyond a simple, probably lust-fueled, infatuation.

Verity held onto the bar and started alternating which foot was en pointe and which was flat against the floor, stretching her calves in the process. It was a simple and mindless exercise she'd done countless of times before and it used to bore her but it seemed to be the only thing that didn't make her head spin.

And given her lack of sleep, her muscles were annoyingly tight, making this exercise as necessary as it was benign. She'd been cycling through it and trying other movements ever since she had arrived back at home after leaving the medical building.

She still had no idea what her father and Zeph were doing but the barre and her newfound physical limitations were keeping her occupied enough that she couldn't let herself worry too much about the unknowns in the whole situation. But she definitely planned on asking her father what was up with him discussing her private medical tests behind her back, especially with Zeph who wasn't related to her, and therefore had no right to know the information.

And what the hell kind of tests came back within minutes? Aside from a pregnancy pee test that anyone could buy at a drugstore, she didn't know of any type of medical test that generated results so fast. Breathalyzer tests for alcohol or marijuana didn't count since those were more for law enforcement purposes than medical. And none of those quick tests involved blood—except whatever they had done to her on the spaceship, which was an unsettling common and recurring theme in her life since her return.

Only minutes had passed since her appointment so there was no way Dr. Lane had already run any of the tests she had claimed to. Which meant Verity had just unwittingly given up four vials of her blood. Everyone seemed to want it, but she still had no idea for what or why.

If she didn't know her father better, she'd worry that he was running some secret genetic study program that the conspiracy theorists were always going on about in addition to supposedly stockpiling the bodies of dead aliens. Neither was accurate, of course, but Verity couldn't stop the paranoid thoughts that were burrowing into her mind with more success than ever before.

Being kidnapped by aliens in the dead of the night would do that to a girl.

ANOTHER HOUR PASSED before Verity heard the front door unlock.

She opened her eyes and got up from her bed. She'd been resting ever since her legs started feeling like jelly. It was probably a sign of her over-stretching but it also felt like how it did when she was walking across the base her first day back. It wasn't natural. The same way her vomiting wasn't.

She slowly walked down the stairs, holding onto the bannister so she wouldn't fall.

Her father looked up at her and frowned.

"You okay?" he asked.

She nodded. Lying to him felt weird but until she knew what he was keeping from her, she wasn't going to share more details with him.

A thought occurred to her, which made her freeze. What if he was secretly listening to her therapy sessions? She would have no way of knowing, but they *were* using his office. The SCIF shouldn't allow for a listening device but she wasn't going to rule out the possibility any more.

Life had kicked her in the teeth with the lesson that anything could happen, so it wasn't a stretch that the government had extra technology that not even the whole base knew about, the same way there were mission details that were compartmentalized to specific individuals and smaller teams.

"How was your check-up?"

"Didn't Dr. Lane tell you?"

His eyebrows raised in surprise.

It took her less than a second to her mistake. She'd inadvertently revealed that she could hear their conversation even though she hadn't been pressing her ear to the door or using a listening device. Something that shouldn't be possible for a human, but clearly it was something she could do.

But now the cat was out of the bag, so there was no reason for her to not ask the question she was dying to: "What anomalies did she find?"

Verity saw and heard her father swallow. She could almost believe him to be uncomfortable, which was an insane possibility. She'd never seen him act like that, even when their home had been invaded.

"There are certain results that have no precedent. We don't know what that means."

"Am I dying?"

"Dr. Lane doesn't think any of them are life-threatening."

"What about my eating?"

"We don't know yet."

"What do you mean? You were talking to her for a long time. What were you doing if that's all you learned?"

"Watch your tone, young lady."

She wanted to scream. Here he was, issuing demands to her like she was a little girl and withholding information about *her* wellbeing as if she couldn't handle the knowledge and be trusted to control her own destiny.

She forced her next words out. "I'm sorry, sir."

"You don't have to 'sir,' me, Verity. You're my daughter."

"Sorry," she echoed.

Though she was acting repentant, she had decided she was anything but and that she needed to become more proactive in getting answers.

18

KNOX

KNOX WAS in the middle of drinking human water when his armor alerted him to a problem from inside the closet.

He wished he had a glass of Eochronian wine. "Ambrosia," as Verity had called it. It was a lot more pleasant than the bland and insubstantial liquid he was currently stuck with.

He placed his glass down on the bedside table and tapped his wrist to disassemble his armor within the closet and instead reform around himself. It was very similar to the technology used in their ships but his use of it now was out of laziness more than necessity.

The armor covered him over his silk sleeping clothes. He'd take it off as soon as he was done checking what was wrong, so he hadn't seen a reason to completely disrobe when he was eventually going to change back into the comfortable garments.

The helmet was the final thing to materialize. A space map was currently projected on the visor. The humans' solar system was displayed as was the location of his ship on Earth and the mothership near what they called Jupiter which was named after a god they had created after encountering one of his kind. But what was truly concerning was the collection of marks that indicated a number of other ships amassing near the Eochronian mothership.

Worse, they were ships his armor recognized. Vruxol, which meant that his kind were no longer in danger only from an insurrectionist, but now an external threat as well.

Once he had become king, he released their Vruxol and Lielneh colonies, promising to not interfere with their affairs as long as they never sought retribution for his ancestors' actions.

It had never been an issue before, but their presence clearly indicated they were done holding up their end of the deal.

He opened a connection to Aerue. Even if his second-in-command was being kept out of the loop by Eiz'm, not even his rival could ignore a warning of an approaching enemy.

Their presence might unfortunately strengthen Eiz'm's bid that military force was the answer to their kind's future, but defending their kind from extinction was a shared goal of everyone, so he couldn't fault Eiz'm in this situation if it meant his soldier effectively defended them.

Knox frowned when Aerue didn't immediately answer. Perhaps he was finally able to participate in a meeting? If so, answering a message from his king would likely antagonize Eiz'm, but even if it was an impromptu turn of events, there were surreptitious ways for Aerue to let him know he was occupied and that he'd get back to him.

The complete lack of answer didn't bode well for what was happening far away from him, and if there was ever a sign he needed to get back there soon, this was it.

He gave up on Aerue and instead contacted Arfilmea.

But she didn't answer either.

He would have worried that perhaps they were in grave trouble like being held captive, or worse, if the enemy ships were close enough to his own to even board his ship. But they were still far out enough that it was an impossibility.

There was the chance that Eiz'm would have imprisoned

Aerue and Arfilmea, but he doubted it. His rival might have installed Dhaca as his right-hand, but there was no way that he could effectively become king without the support of the remaining nobility, especially when one of them was the true king's fiancée. Without her support, his hold would be tenuous at best, and executing her would likely anger the council so much that they would abandon the coup and instead oust Eiz'm, which would serve him right but Knox didn't want Arfilmea to be caught in the middle of a fight that she hadn't picked.

He hadn't picked it either, but he was a main player, whether he wanted to be or not. Unfortunately, as his second-in-command, Aerue was involved, too, but it seemed Eiz'm was ignoring issues rather than directly challenging which was a blessing in disguise.

At least when he returned, his allies wouldn't be dead, their corpses likely thrown into space to freeze to prevent any chance of resuscitation. Depending on the manner of execution, it would be impossible anyway, but Knox hoped it wasn't a necessary concern.

He contacted one of his soldiers in space, and finally got through. Knox couldn't tell where she was but it certainly wasn't near Eiz'm for her to be answering.

"Yes, Your Majesty?"

Knox checked to see if there were any signs of insincerity in her expression or tone of voice but found none. At least there were some people on board who still respected the crown.

"There are Vruxilian ships amassing near you. Alert whoever you need to defend our home." He didn't want to let her know that he knew of the attempted coup in case she *was* exceptionally good at lying and was doing so right now. Otherwise, he would have said Aerue, and nothing might have happened, or he would have said, "tell Eiz'm" and that would reveal that he knew what was going on in his absence.

There was a very good chance that Eiz'm had recruited the

soldiers first before going after the council, making sure he had the physical back up he needed to make his play for the throne.

"Yes, Your Majesty. Will you be returning soon?"

"Yes," he said. But he didn't give a time frame because doing so would allow a trap to be set upon his arrival.

There was also the small detail that he still had no idea what he was going to do about leaving Earth and the two best candidates for his project behind.

He could ask Zeph his advice since Aerue was becoming less and less of an option given his unavailability and limited knowledge of Eiz'm's plans.

There was a possibility that Zeph *could* get the human captain and let him in so he could personally get Verity, but again, breaking into the base while they were expecting it wasn't the easiest option.

He should have taken the opportunity to snatch her when she was at school. At least then, he'd have her and he wouldn't have to deal with being framed for her guard's murder—they'd already be heading back to his ship together if that had been the case.

Knox shed his armor and stored it into the container that was about the size of a small coin and slipped it into his silk pocket.

He tilted his head and listened for Zeph. It didn't sound like he had his boyfriend over, but he wanted to be sure it was just the two of them before he went in to talk to his agent.

Another moment passed and he could only hear Zeph breathing in his room.

Knox stood and knocked on his agent's door. He could have contacted him the same way he did with the others of their kind but given he was right next door, there was no real reason to use the technology.

"Come in!" The voice was too quiet for a human to hear but it was clear for his ears.

Knox opened the door and saw Zeph sit up quickly from his bed.

"What do you need, Your Majesty?"

"Did I interrupt something?"

His agent shook his head.

"Then why do you look like I did?"

"I was video chatting with my boyfriend."

"I didn't hear anything."

"We had each other on mute and were just watching each other sleep." His agent gave him a knowing smile.

"What does having the communication on mute accomplish?"

"We just get to spend time together."

"I'm sorry I cut into your time. But this is an urgent matter."

"There's no reason for you to apologize, Your Majesty. I'm here to serve you. What do you need?"

"There are Vruxilian ships surrounding our mothership. I need you to contact anyone you can aboard the ship to let them know. Do not tell them that I told you to."

"Yes, Your Majesty. Is there a reason you don't want me to say I'm acting on your orders?"

"Things are… complicated right now," he said. "Right now, we just have to act in the best interest of our kind, and that shouldn't require your actions being a result of a royal order."

If his agent had more questions, he didn't voice them.

"Do it now, please."

"What are you going to do?"

"Go for a walk." Isn't that what humans did when they needed to clear their minds and get a new perspective on things? "I'll let you know if I need anything else from you."

"Yes, Your Majesty."

Knox went back to his room, donned his armor, and left the house with the invisibility turned on.

For once, he wasn't going toward the base or directly to the strip. Instead, he just walked down the street past the other houses, taking in how they were all copies of each other. Two floors, triangular roofs, and white doors.

Idyllic, as the humans would say.

And they had no idea the danger that he and Zeph posed to them, though they were much better off with the two of them than if he had ever been reckless enough to send Eiz'm undercover. Though, if he had, he wouldn't be in his current position. Then again, the humans on the planet would already probably be dying off at an alarming rate due to Eiz'm's warpath.

Human's called such murders *serial killers* but he doubted they would ever be able to recognize a pattern if Eiz'm were killing them.

At least he hadn't ever had such a bad lapse in judgement that would cause him to send his trigger-happy official to Earth.

In retrospect, he probably should have never let him near the humans for collection or interrogation purposes, but at least he had saved Verity from his abuse.

Zeph hadn't said anything about her complaining about her ribs so he had to assume his healing serum had done its job but perhaps he should give her more.

Aerue would likely don his most disapproving expression if he knew but as Knox was the king, he could decide what he did with his personal supply.

Knox pulled out the small vial and considered it. A few drops in her drink should do the trick but she wasn't someone who kept a personal liquid container near her at all times. If he put it into the water supply, he couldn't guarantee it would get to her and not someone else by accident.

Eochronian technology was advanced, but not enough to accomplish that, unfortunately.

Zeph had also told him that the human doctor on base had found multiple anomalies in the tests they'd run on her earlier that day.

Knox knew that they wouldn't be able to effectively identify what those meant before his plan could move into the next stage, but their awareness of the physical changes was something to consider in speeding up the process to get ahead of their discovery timeline.

He'd have to contact Dr. Mak'en for a status report on the other subjects. Perhaps he would get lucky and they would have shown exponential improvement in his absence.

But even if Verity's changed percentages were due to sharing meals with him, he couldn't very well order the same delicacies be served to the humans. Even if he were aboard the ship, his staff would object and without him there, there was no way to enforce the edict without likely inciting a riot and only further lending credence to Eiz'm's campaign.

Knox shook his head.

His head was miles away with his kind and trying to fight his challenger while he suspected his heart was only a short run for him, sleeping soundly in her bedroom with the protection of the one man he couldn't stand more than any other human.

It was a mess of massive proportions and for all their evolutionary benefits over humans, he found himself at such an emotional loss that one would think he was no better than the indecisive and weak beings who were normally, ironically, and unfortunately put into positions of power on this planet.

He doubted his grandfather would ever allow for such hesitant and vacillating behavior, and his father would have likely told him that taking care of their own should rightfully be the priority—but couldn't his kind see that his project was doing just that?

If the Vruxol weren't about to attack them, perhaps he could convince the council and others who doubted him, but the longer he stayed here, the more he destroyed his credibility with his dissenters.

Maybe it was past time he go home, but he wasn't quite ready to leave just yet.

He needed to talk to her. Based on her Verity's growing frustration and confusion, he bet that the spitfire would be visiting Trohm soon to demand answers.

And while he could easily get that report from either of his agents stationed here, he wanted to be here in case she took it one step further and sought him out.

He wouldn't put it past her and he was secretly hoping she would. At least, then, he'd be able to see her, talk to her, and then he could whisk them away to deal with his other problems.

It was still a plan that predicated on an unfortunate number of hypothesis and hopes but she had yet to disappoint him, even as he was sure she had tried to in the past by discouraging his invitations to dine with him. But she had eventually acquiesced, even if it were a guise to escape.

He would stay put for now, and then reevaluate once she had made her next move.

19

VERITY

VERITY CHECKED HER PHONE. It read four in the morning but instead of calling Ben up to her room again to help her sleep, she silently got dressed and tiptoed downstairs. It was officially McDonald's turn to keep watch, and she wasn't surprised when he intercepted her at the stairs.

"What are you doing?" he asked.

She held a finger up to her lips, and he waited for her to put on her shoes.

She unlocked the door and motioned for him to follow. She silently locked it and hoped that neither her father nor Ben heard it.

Both of them normally woke up at five, so she should be safe, but she didn't want to take any chances.

She led McDonald away from her home. Before he could stop her, she marched toward the building where she was almost positive they were keeping Trohm. She started running, and found herself moving faster than she ever had.

Before she knew it, she was already almost to her destination.

She stopped before she could collide with the building and turned to see McDonald running after her.

"What are you doing?" he asked again, once he caught up, this time at a normal volume level now that they were no longer inside with two sleeping people.

"Going to talk to him."

"Are you crazy? Your dad will kill me if I let that happen."

"You're not *letting* anything happen. You're just not going to snitch."

"Why am I always keeping secrets? First Tenner in your room and now this? I didn't ask for this!"

She almost pitied him. "You'll be fine. Now, shush."

She stared at the guards who were patrolling the area.

The one in front took a step towards her, a hand on his gun and ready to go. "No visitors allowed."

"I'm the General's daughter."

"Doesn't matter."

"Captain Tenner spoke to him yesterday."

The man neither confirmed nor denied the statement, so Verity guessed she finally had her answer. He had definitely come to talk to Trohm.

"He's not going to talk," the man finally said.

"He will to me. He owes me."

The guard didn't look convinced.

"Just let me see him," she said, wishing she could influence his mind like superheroes and supernatural creatures could.

As if she had willed it, the man relaxed, and entered the pin code to let her in.

She didn't bother to turn around and see McDonald's probably shocked expression.

Verity slipped inside and saw a barren first floor with an elevator and stairway. She had expected something, but it wasn't this.

She went to the stairwell door and opened it. They only headed down, so she followed them into the dark.

The moment she reached the basement, a bunch of fluorescent lights lit up, revealing Trohm sitting in a chair at the far end of the hallway behind glass.

She saw a door behind him but had no idea how to get to it.

For now, she'd be stuck talking to him through the glass.

As she got closer, she realized it was so clean that it almost looked invisible but it was actually pretty thick when she looked at it from an angle.

She let out a breath she hadn't realized she was holding. A part of her had been worried that the glass had been removed the way it had been in a TV show where that very thing had happened to the disadvantage of the protagonist.

Even though the aliens were stronger than humans, she bet it would still take considerable force to break through.

And that would be assuming Trohm could break out of the metal chair holding him by the wrists and ankles. There was no way the restraints were as strong as the ones she'd been stuck in but maybe there was a chance they were strong enough to hold him for a bit. They looked to be made of titanium so there was a chance but she had a feeling Trohm was simply biding his time and could have easily broken out on the first day if he had wanted to.

The question was, what was he waiting for?

The bastard was smiling at her, and she suddenly had the sense that it wasn't a *what* he'd been waiting for but a *whom*. Her.

"About time you got here."

"Do you know how hard it is to get here without my father or Ben knowing?"

"I can only imagine."

He was entirely too smug for a man who was imprisoned. He was definitely sticking around by choice instead of by force.

"How'd you manage it?"

"Wouldn't you like to know?"

If he was going to be a cryptic ass, she could be cagey, too.

Verity turned and saw a chair sitting in the corner near the glass divider. She grabbed it and turned it so she could sit and watch him.

Even though the setting was a little like when the young FBI agent met with the infamous serial killer in the Oscar-winning movie adaptation of the award-winning and chilling thriller novel. But unlike that scenario, the glass here didn't have large breathing holes cut into them, or a tray that could be used to transport items from visitor to prisoner or vice versa.

But she didn't want anything he could give her. Nothing physical, anyway.

"Are you just going to stare me to death?" Trohm asked. "Because I have to warn you, my kind have a very extended life-span in comparison to your short human century. You'd expire long before me."

"Good to know." Knox hadn't outright said that as much though he'd hinted at when he said he was young for his kind but old for hers, but it was nice to finally have concrete information about the aliens.

They already knew so much about humans that she was stuck playing catch up.

If Trohm hadn't meant to let that slip and realized his mistake, he didn't show any alarm.

But she couldn't imagine why Trohm, or perhaps more accurately, Knox would suddenly want her to know more about their race. Especially when he'd been so unwilling to answer her questions on the very same topic when they were together in space.

"So," she leaned back in the chair to balance herself on the edge of the seat, "exactly how old are you? In human years, please."

"Twenty-five-million, give or take a few centuries."

Her jaw dropped open before she could stop it.

Her first time had been with an *alien* who was *millions* of years old?

Verity suddenly felt the urge to throw up again but doing so would only let whoever came in to interrogate Trohm next that someone else had been here. She took a deep breath through her nose and swallowed slowly, forcing the bile to go back down where it belonged.

Trohm sent her another smile. "Pretty good performance from a guy my age, right?"

"Disgusting."

"Hey, it's not any creepier than all those paranormal romance novels with vampires and high school girls. And at least you were a legal adult when we hooked up."

She wanted to smack him. Even though it was just the two of them, she had no guarantee there weren't any listening devices planted to record his interrogation sessions. What if her father heard that admission?

"I was drunk. So were you."

"I guess I should take the time now to admit that my kind can't become intoxicated on human libations."

"So, not only did you lie about who you were, what you are, and your age, but you also took advantage of a drunk girl while you were completely sober?" She couldn't help that her voice was getting louder with each grievance in the list but it was a little hard to stay calm when you learn that a close betrayal only went deeper and got worse.

He raised an eyebrow. "That's not fair."

"You're kidding me. You want to talk about—"

"If you remembered correctly, you'd recall that I asked you *multiple* times if you wanted to continue throughout our encounter. I would've stopped had you said to. But you never did."

She couldn't respond to that. Despite being drunk, she *did* remember that. And she hadn't felt pressured by him at all at the time, either. It was a consensual encounter... with the information she had at the time. It was such a fucked up situation.

She cleared her throat and changed the topic. "So, I'm assuming you know what your king has planned for me?"

Trohm tilted his head. "You could say that."

"Does he know what we did? Or did you keep that little tidbit from him?"

His smug expression finally dropped.

Verity would have laughed if it weren't such a serious topic.

These creatures had been playing god with her life for years on end without her knowing. And it was bad enough when she learned the hard way that not all of the aliens were on the same page when Eiz'm was beating up on her against his king's orders. But to know that her first contact with them—in any capacity, not just the carnal one—was also acting rogue, hurt in an unimaginable way. At least her physical injuries could heal. But if she could ever trust her own judgment again, it would be a miracle.

That's what the therapy was for, and while it helped her not completely freak out in her subsequent fight classes, it wasn't doing anything to make her less paranoid on a daily basis or help her sleep better yet.

And maybe time would heal all her wounds, her mental ones in addition to her physical ones, but she couldn't wait for that time to arrive. If only there were a fast-forward button. She had seen a movie as a kid about that very wish being fulfilled with disastrous results but she couldn't imagine it really being a problem. She wouldn't be skipping ahead during every personal moment to the point that the remote thought she didn't want to live life, even the more mundane moments. Was it too much to ask that she not have to deal with the trauma but have already *dealt* with it?

"So, have you started experiencing stuff yet?"

She leaned forward, resting her elbows on her knees. "What do you mean?"

"Increased strength, speed, you know—what you humans call *superhuman* abilities."

"Well, I'm sorry we got the term wrong. Though, to be fair, some people say inhuman for that, too. And your kind has definitely been *inhumane* to us."

"How's Wells doing?"

"Fine," she snapped. In reality, she had no idea but no one had reported anything going wrong with his recovery so she assumed she was right. Even if she wasn't, there was no reason for the traitor to know the truth.

"Can you still handle human food?"

"Are you saying you can't? I've seen you eat it before without a problem."

Trohm shrugged behind the glass. "But it doesn't offer me any nutrients. The taste doesn't do much for me either."

"But why can't I keep it down?"

"Don't know."

He seemed so sincere but she didn't believe him. How could he not know? He'd been watching her for years.

"Do you have any regrets?"

"About sleeping with you?" Trohm was back to being a snarky ass. "None at all. You were pretty enthusiastic."

"I meant about lying to me." She almost admitted that she had cared about him but swallowed the words before they could escape. She didn't bother dignifying the second statement with a response. It would only encourage him.

He didn't verbally answer, but she could almost swear she saw a glint of regret in his eyes. Or maybe it was a trick of the light. It didn't matter. What was done was done, and she knew she couldn't trust him again. And she could recognize that he wasn't going to share anything else with her.

She stood up and left without saying goodbye.

Let him rot in the basement for all she cared.

When she exited the building, McDonald was standing exactly where she'd left him. But next to him stood Ben and her father, both wearing matching forbidding expressions.

Well, shit.

20

KNOX

KNOX CRUSHED the speaker in his hand.

He'd been listening to Trohm and Verity's conversation, and his satisfaction at having correctly predicted her behavior had quickly given way to a growing and increasingly urgent need to punch his own undercover agent.

Verity had been right to guess that Trohm hadn't told him about their liaison. From the sound of their conversation, it was obviously a secret they had kept from the humans but for his agent to have not told him was an egregious oversight in his reporting.

And incredibly dangerous, given Trohm's behavior could very well have endangered Verity's life before she was even ready to become a viable subject in his program. At that point in time, it was only a vague possibility. There had always been a chance at some point that something would go wrong and the human subjects would weed themselves out before they were collected through unforeseen and unpredicted circumstances.

But the fact that none of the subjects who were under observation were disqualified was interesting on its own. It was the proof he'd shown his council when pitching his plan as not only possible but highly viable.

But that wasn't his main concern now. He was only concerned with one subject, the same one he'd been preoccupied with ever since he met her.

And to learn that his agent had had her while he hadn't because he'd been worried about hurting her made him positively furious. With Trohm, Verity, himself, the situation. Nothing was going how he wanted it to, but there was only so much he could do to change the circumstances.

At the very least, he'd be treating Trohm to another visit.

He needed to have this conversation face to face, and perhaps even get in a good punch or two. It would be justified, after all.

Knox turned on the invisibility capabilities of his armor as he stepped out of his room.

His head was still visible when he ran into Zeph, who asked, "Is there an emergency, Your Majesty?"

"No," he said. "I'm just going to get another status report from Trohm."

His agent wisely didn't comment on the fact that he could hear the listening end of the bug he had planted where their fellow Eochronian was being held captive.

Knox quickly made his way onto base, and instead of fighting the guards again, he caused a distraction at the back of the building, forcing the man there to call in reinforcements from the others, to leave the front unguarded long enough for him to sneak in.

His agent refused to meet his gaze when he walked up to the glass.

If Trohm truly were a human as he'd been pretending for the past fourteen years, he might have been surprised to see his king so soon without any warning, but Knox knew that Trohm could hear him approaching before he even reached the building.

"You certainly left out a few things during your reports over the years."

His agent was silent.

"When exactly did you…" there were multiple human terms for what they had done but any of them were so shocking that they brought to mind images he didn't want to be seeing—even if they were only in his imagination—"have your relations with her?"

"Her twenty-first birthday."

So, only last year.

It was still much too long for his agent to have kept such a very important detail from him, but at least he hadn't been hiding it for over a human decade.

Knox forced his voice to stay level as he asked his next question. "Did you take advantage of her?"

If he had, there would be hell to pay—as the humans said. Consent was a mandatory aspect in all carnal relations among Eochronians, a concept that was strangely difficult for humanity to grasp.

Trohm finally met his gaze. "No, Your Majesty. I would never do that. I even waited until she had sobered up first. And I asked her multiple times throughout the night if she wanted to continue. I thought she was lucid."

His answer involved more thinking about their liaison but Knox was relieved to hear that his agent hadn't done anything untoward when it came to consent.

But that didn't change the fact that Trohm had jeopardized Verity's viability for his program.

Knox let the silence drag out before he finally demanded, "What were you thinking?"

If she had somehow gotten pregnant from their encounter, there was a very good chance she could have died, or at the very least become infertile—for both human and Eochronian reproduction.

And while he understood not every female wanted to become a mother—take Arfilmea for example—having a choice medically taken away from you was always different than personally deciding what to do with one's body.

Trohm cleared his throat. "She came onto me."

"You should have turned her down."

"She would have just gone on to one of the other people on the base."

"But that wouldn't have significant repercussions." At least, not for them. Accidental pregnancies happened for humans all the time, though he suspected Verity would have been careful even if she was under the influence of alcohol.

Knox shook his head. He didn't like thinking about all these potential results of Verity's sexual behavior. Never mind that they were all in the past and obviously hadn't come to fruition. Thinking of her with *anyone* wasn't pleasant.

He forced his next words out. "How many times?"

"Just the one."

"Trohm—"

"I swear, Your Majesty. We never brought it up again. She didn't want anyone to know."

Understandable. At least he now knew that she hadn't tried to turn it into an ongoing affair.

"She might consider it a careless mistake but I don't think she regrets it."

Knox didn't answer. He didn't really need to know that. Not that he would have wished Verity to regret her first carnal experience, but knowing that it was something she enjoyed with his undercover agent wasn't exactly welcome news to him.

"She never suspected you weren't human before she unmasked you?"

Trohm shook his head. "No one did. I'm sorry I failed in maintaining my cover. I had no idea she would be able to do that."

Neither had he. To operate any Eochronian technology should have been beyond a human's capability but Verity wasn't a normal human. Her being able to read Eochronian to operate the escape pod she had commandeered for her escape was proof enough of that, even if he hadn't understand the extent of her abilities at the time.

She hadn't given any indication of being able to do that while she was aboard the ship but there was every possibility that she had gained the talent earlier and merely concealed it. Verity wasn't one to tip her hand early and letting any of his guards know that their language wasn't a secret certainly could be qualified as such.

He had been equally careful in keeping details about his plan and his kind a secret. He hadn't particularly minded that Trohm had finally shared a more concrete age with her, though he still would have preferred she be kept in the dark. The less the humans knew about their kind, the better. And any information given to Verity, being as intelligent as she was, was in some way handing her a weapon to use against them.

A small part of him also didn't want her to know their age gap because it would inherently change the way she looked at him.

He knew they would never be equal, but he didn't want their differences to dictate everything about their relationship.

Knox could practically hear her voice saying, "Kidnapping me ruined any chance of that."

Perhaps she was right, but he wouldn't accept it until he absolutely had to.

"There are Vruxilian ships approaching our ship. I need you go to back and handle the situation with Aerue."

"Isn't he already handling the situation?"

"Just give him back up. I'll be following soon, but not quite yet."

Perhaps he should send Zephyr back, too.

"Yes, Your Majesty."

Knox nodded, and pulled up the frequency in his armor necessary to break his agent out.

"Cover your ears," he warned.

He plugged his own ears with his helmet and pressed his hands to the glass. Then he started playing the incredibly high-pitched frequency. Their advanced hearing unfortunately made them susceptible to the sound. He ran from one end of the glass to the other, allowing the frequency to vibrate through his hands and through the glass until he could see the clear material start to shake. He could have stayed still but doing it this way distributed the force more evenly and got the job done faster.

The moment it shattered, Trohm broke out of his restraints, ripping through the titanium as if it were nothing more than a weak metalloid. Knox waited for Trohm to don his Eochronian armor, and together, they rushed out of the building and off the air base.

Trohm followed Knox to Zephyr's home, and they didn't slow down until after they were safely inside.

Zephyr came out of his bedroom and took them both in. "I missed the jailbreak?"

"It was an impromptu decision," Knox confessed.

"You weren't going to let me out?" Trohm asked.

"I always planned to at some point, but I wasn't going to for a bit longer, but the situation with the Vruxols needs to be dealt with. Zephyr, you and Trohm need to leave as soon as possible."

"Yes, Your Majesty," both of them answered, though he could detect some sadness in his host's expression.

"You may say goodbye to your boyfriend," Knox said. "But the sooner you can leave, the better."

He hadn't yet checked the space map again to see whether their enemy had gotten closer but he needed as many allies on the ship as possible to help defend their people and also stem the rebellion before it got completely out of hand.

"Trohm," he said, "I've set up a star filtering system in the guest room. I recommend you use it to regain your strength."

His agent nodded. "Thank you, Your Majesty." He left to do just that.

"May I be excused, Your Majesty?" Zephyr asked. "I'd like to visit my boyfriend before I leave."

"Yes, you may. I do apologize for the necessity. Perhaps when things calm down, you can come back and resume your relationship."

Though his program was predicated on procreating with humans, he wasn't going to force all of his kind to participate if they were already in committed relationships.

Polyamory, as the humans called it, was not uncommon among his kind, nor was bisexuality or even pansexuality but cheating was just as heinous to them as it was to the people on this planet. Even more so, given the frequency of the phenomenon on Earth and the rarity of it among his own kind, given the steep penalty or public humiliation for both guilty parties.

But he wouldn't be sharing any of his partners with anyone. Arfilmea and him had an understanding, but no one would ever touch Verity unless it was him.

Now that he was sending his physically closest allies far away, the time was fast approaching that he needed to see her again before he had to rejoin his people.

And in that moment, he decided she would be joining him on that voyage.

He wasn't leaving this planet's atmosphere without her, whether she liked it or not.

21

VERITY

"I'M SORRY," McDonald said.

"It's not your fault," Verity replied as she was walked away between her father and Ben, not unlike how Trohm had been taken away by the STFs when they had returned home a few days ago.

He trailed behind them.

She glanced back over her shoulder and saw that he was keeping his gaze on the ground in front of him.

She turned back around and did the same, unable to meet her father or Ben's gazes as they all marched back to the house.

Once they arrived, Verity waited with Ben for her father to unlock the home.

She sat down on the living room couch while the three men stared down at her. Her father stood directly in front of her while Ben was at his right side and McDonald was on his left.

Verity braced herself for the lecture but was surprised when her father first addressed the young STF.

"You're lucky I don't demote you for such a lack of judgment. What the hell were you thinking, letting her go talk to it?"

Wow, her dad was pissed. He wasn't even giving Trohm the

benefit of having a name or being a living organism. He'd rendered the alien mole an *it*.

The STF was smart and didn't say anything other than, "I'm sorry, sir."

Verity felt bad. She'd have to make it up to him somehow.

Maybe set him up on a date with one of her dancer classmates once she no longer needed him as a guard. Though, who knew how long that would be?

She was pretty sure she'd just extended that period indefinitely by pulling this stunt.

"And you," her father said, finally turning his full attention onto her, "what the hell were you thinking? Slipping past your guards to secretly talk to someone who could kill you?"

"He was stuck behind the glass. It's not like he could do anything from that side."

"You don't know that," her father snapped. "You're lucky nothing happened. Why would you put yourself in danger like that?"

"I wanted answers. You certainly weren't giving me any."

She saw both Ben and McDonald look down at the floor when she said that, even before her father replied.

"Watch your tone, young lady."

"I'm twenty-two, dad. I'm not six. And you weren't being straight with me about a lot of things, so I figured there wasn't any harm in asking him."

"You didn't think it would be a problem to ask the truth from someone who you know has lied to you on a regular basis for years on end?"

"At least if he lied, I would expect it. But I never thought you'd keep secrets from me like you have been since I returned."

Her father just stared at her. Maybe he was shocked at how much she was talking back, or maybe he was surprised she had picked up on his lying, or maybe it was something else. But he was currently silently willing her to give in.

She met his gaze and refused to back down. Blinking first would be admitting defeat, and she wasn't going to do that.

Verity had never rebelled, despite everyone warning her father that she would, and people making some inappropriate comments about him probably wishing her mother was still alive to handle a hormonal teenage girl.

But in the short five days that she'd been home since crashing back through the atmosphere, she'd pushed against his edicts more than she had in her whole life—unless you count when she was five and kept begging for a silly digital pet that was more of a time suck than a way to teach responsibility, as she had tried to position it.

She could feel her eyes starting to get dry, but she forced her eyes wider to counteract the instinct to close her lids. She knew the biological reason for why, but sometimes it truly was an instance of mind over matter.

Finally, her father looked away and she silently high-fived herself for the little victory. She was sure everyone in the room knew it represented more than a simple staring contest but no one voiced the expanded significance.

Her father didn't say another word as he turned on his heel and walked out of the room. She heard him walk up the stairs, and stayed seated on the couch.

Ben sat next to her, and McDonald took that as a silent cue to leave the room.

She heard him move into the security room and kept her gaze forward, still unable to look Ben in the eye.

"So," he said. "You talked to him?"

She nodded. "So did you."

He didn't answer.

"That's where you snuck off to yesterday, right?"

He gave a noncommittal grunt, but she knew it was a confirmation of her suspicion.

"What did you talk to him about?" she asked.

"I should be asking you that. Do you know how panicked your father was once he realized you weren't in your bedroom?"

She forced a light tone. "Are you saying you weren't worried about me?"

"That's not what I meant, and you know it."

Neither of them said anything for a beat.

"You didn't answer the question," she finally prompted again when she couldn't take the silence anymore.

"I talked to him about how he lied to us the whole time. You?"

"Same."

"There has to be more. You said you wanted answers about what was happening to you."

There was something strange in his tone. She turned to see his face as she asked, "Don't you?"

He shrugged. "Of course, I do, but I'm not going to trust him."

"Then I guess you don't want to hear what he said."

"You're putting words in my mouth."

She didn't answer him, immediately. She didn't want to be interrogated by him, and even though they were sitting together on the couch in her living room, it was the same type of power-dynamic she'd been forced to have with Aerue once he had taken over Eiz'm's role, minus the truth serum.

He sighed. "What did he say?"

"He's twenty-five million years old."

Ben let out a low whistle.

Verity knew how he felt. If she had been able to, she probably would have done the same thing when she was talking to Trohm.

It seemed like it was somehow a mandatory skill in the STFs on the base. She'd yet to meet one who couldn't whistle. Kind of like she'd never seen an actor unable to wink. Maybe it was just part of the job.

"What else?"

"Human food doesn't taste like much or give them nutrition. He also doesn't know why I can't keep food down."

"Do you believe him?"

"I couldn't think of a good reason for him to lie about that specifically."

"Still doesn't mean he was telling the truth."

"Look, if you're really so skeptical, why don't you go interrogate him again? You can take me along, too."

He laughed drily. "Nice try. But I'm not dumb enough to fall for that. But I might pay him another visit."

Just as he finished talking, she heard her father curse loudly upstairs.

Ben shot up from the couch and ran to the stairs.

She started to follow, but he pushed her back down onto the couch.

"Hey!" she objected, bouncing on the cushion once due to the force of her landing.

He didn't look back as he said, "Stay down here. McDonald, cover her! I'm going upstairs to check on the General."

"Yes, sir," she heard McDonald say before he even reentered the living room.

She heard Ben run up the stairs and heavy footsteps meet him.

Verity hoped like hell it was just her father, and not an intruder who was waiting to ambush Ben.

No fight broke out, so she assumed everything was okay. A hunch that was further confirmed when she heard her father talking to Ben at the top of the stairs.

"He escaped," her father said in a low voice.

Verity got up and ran to the base of the stairs before McDonald could stop her. Though she wasn't a fan of the forceful experimentation done on her, the newfound speed she'd been given was proving useful.

Her eyes darting to the door. Was it about to burst open, or would he be hiding like his king clearly was? And if he came after her, would she have to fight him again? Would he hurt McDonald or Ben?

She swallowed the lump in her throat and choked out, "Trohm is gone?"

Both men turned to stare at her, probably wondering how she'd heard that tidbit of information.

"Glass shattered, no one saw anything."

"Were the cameras disabled?"

"No."

Her father continued down the steps, Ben following him.

"I need to call an emergency meeting. The three of you stay here. You can call my assistant to order in food. No one leaves under any circumstances, and don't open any windows or doors until I come back."

His tone and speed of talking didn't leave any chance to argue, and he was out the door only a moment later.

She stared at the shut door and held in the sigh that rose to her lips.

She went back to the living room and plopped down on the couch. House arrest sucked.

ONCE THEY ARRIVED HOME, Verity ran upstairs to her bedroom, leaving the men downstairs. She had almost completely closed the door before McDonald snuck his hand in, blocking it.

"What?" she demanded.

"Door has to stay open."

"I'm about to have a private conversation with my therapist."

He looked uncomfortable.

"Can I close my door if you stay outside in the hall? I can give you my desk chair to make it more comfortable." It would fill up most of the hallway but then at least she could pretend she wasn't being eavesdropped on while she talked to Dr. Hudson.

She stared at him while he debated in his head. She could practically see the gears turning as he weighed the pros and cons of her proposed compromise, and whether or not he'd get in trouble again for listening to her.

"Let me check your windows first."

She rolled her eyes but opened the door to let him in. Did he honestly think she was going to sneak out of the house with him on the other side of the door?

That would just be stupid. At least when she was going to talk to Trohm earlier that day, she had enlisted his help because she knew that sneaking past all three men in the house was unrealistic.

And her father had raised her to be a pragmatist over her mother's more optimistic personality. If she had lived longer, maybe Verity would have grown into an optimistic realist or a realistic optimist but it was what it was.

McDonald shoved the windows up, and then down. They didn't budge.

"Well?" she demanded. It was getting close to her appointment time and while she didn't have a commute to worry about, she didn't want to be late to her first phone session.

She'd texted Dr. Hudson the moment it was clear she was stuck inside all day and the woman had luckily been very understanding.

When it was proposed they do a video chat, that was shut down by Ben who cited it being a bad idea to give anyone a digital view into the house.

She didn't believe her psychiatrist to be another alien mole but she couldn't prove that she *wasn't* so she just accepted Ben's decision.

McDonald turned to her. "Okay. But I reserve the right to come in here if I hear anything suspicious on your side of the door."

"Okay, okay. Can you go now?"

She glanced at her phone. It was the exact time of her

appointment which meant Dr. Hudson would be calling any moment now.

He left and she shut the door fast, just as her phone rang with the incoming call.

She hit answer. "Hello?"

"Hello, Verity. Am I calling at a good time or do you need to reschedule?"

She sat down on her bed, propped up against the pillows. "Why would you say that?"

"You sound a little out of breath. Is everything okay on your end? I know your need to make this session virtual was very sudden, too."

"Everything is fine," Verity said, automatically.

"What do we say about the word fine?"

"It means *feelings inside not expressed*." Verity rolled her eyes. It was one of those silly acronyms that you expected elementary kids to know the same way they learned the order of the planets with that ridiculous mnemonic which was no longer even accurate now that Pluto had been reclassified as a dwarf planet.

Forcing her, an adult, to recite the silly acronym made her feel like a child but she had to admit it was annoyingly effective.

"So, please tell me how you're really feeling."

"Anxious."

"Tell me more about it."

"I just got some news that... my abductor may be nearby." It wasn't strictly untrue but she had known that ever since coming out of her shower a few days ago.

And while she knew Trohm hadn't specifically abducted her—she had seen him lined up with the other captured humans that night—he was partially responsible for it.

"I see," Dr. Hudson responded.

Verity doubted that very much.

"Have you found yourself being extra hyper vigilant since learning this information?"

Extra was hard to quantify. She'd been full-throttle vigilant since she learned Knox was out there somewhere, close enough to leave her love notes on her pillow, and moving too fast for them to catch him.

A part of her was surprised Trohm had waited until she was gone to break out. Wouldn't it have made more sense for him to do it while she was there and just grab her and go?

She had no idea *where* he was going, but she doubted he was sticking around now that the whole base was on high alert for him as well as his king.

"You could say that," she said.

"I understand there may be things you are not ready to share, and perhaps even things you *cannot* share with me, Verity, but I need you to be as descriptive with your language as possible so I can understand your state of mind and thought processes as you're answering my questions."

Verity sighed, and settled further back into her pillows.

If she was going to be open about her emotions, it was going to take a while.

"I'm confused."

"About what?"

If she'd demanded an answer, Verity would've bristled but Dr. Hudson's voice was more calming than probing.

"Sometimes I'm scared and other times I'm fi—feel almost normal," she corrected before the psychiatrist could.

"Normal how?"

"I don't think about the constant danger I'm in. And other than having to do fight classes again, not going to school, and my father insisting I be guarded, my life isn't different on a day to day basis. Almost like summer break."

"What are those like? Just you and your dad?"

"Yeah."

"You've lived with him your whole life?"

"Yes." What did this have to do with anything?

"How do you feel about that?"

"What do you mean?"

"Your father has recently instituted some safety precautions, yes?"

"How did you feel about them?"

"Annoyed but I understand why."

"Has he ever annoyed you before?"

"Of course he has. He's human." Unlike her attackers, though they obviously annoyed her, too.

"You're twenty-two. Did you ever want to move out once you became an adult? When you started college?"

"Yeah. I had to convince him to even let me go. And I had to stay in state."

"Have you ever asked him why?"

"He's not big on giving answers for his rules."

"I see."

"See what?"

"Have you ever heard of individuation?"

"No."

"It's a natural process of a child becoming more independent and their own person apart from their parents. Do you have any feelings about it?"

"Well, I'm independent."

"In what ways?"

"I can take care of myself. Kidnapping notwithstanding, of course."

"Have you ever wanted more independence?"

"I never really thought about it after the college discussion— or the my recent house arrest."

It felt good to talk about it but it also felt a little like a betrayal of her dad.

"I don't have a bad relationship with him," she added. "He's just protective."

"And recent events haven't helped him let go of the idea that you're his daughter and need his protection."

"Right."

Dr. Hudson didn't say anything for a moment and Verity assumed she was writing something down.

"I want to return to your definition of normal."

"What about it?" Hadn't they already covered that ground?

"You're worried that you sometimes feel that way even though you're still in danger. I want you to know that it's not necessarily a bad thing."

"It's ignoring the reality of my situation. Or, at least forgetting it temporarily."

"It's too soon to talk about diagnoses for you, but your symptoms are understandably distressing."

"Your point?" Verity winced at the sharpness in her voice. "Sorry—"

"Thank you, but there's no need to apologize. I understand that we're covering a lot of topics. It's not uncommon for people to clam up after a lot of sharing."

"Still, I was rude."

"I want you to also know that it's a *good* thing that it's not constantly on your mind. It means that your life isn't fully consumed by what happened. Our goal isn't that you forget history but that it doesn't adversely affect your daily life to a debilitating degree."

"So, I'm making progress?"

"Verity, progress for therapy isn't linear. And we've been speaking for five days. It's too soon to tell. Do you have anything else on your mind right now?"

Being scared of being pregnant with an alien baby wasn't something she could say. Or that she suspected her doctor was doing something behind her back, or her father was keeping classified secrets.

"No," she said.

There was a knock on her door.

"Thank you so much, Dr. Hudson," she said and hung up.

"Come in."

McDonald stuck his head in. "Everything okay?"

She nodded, then yawned, feeling suddenly drained of energy. "I'm going to take a nap," she said.

He nodded. "I'll let Ben and your father know." He closed the door, leaving it cracked open.

She turned off her bedroom light and crawled under the covers.

Hopefully, she'd be able to get rest without more nightmares but she wasn't hopeful.

22

KNOX

KNOX WASN'T EXPECTING a message from his agents once they were safely aboard the mothership. But the Vruxilian threat had him opening Trohm's communication immediately, desperate for information.

"Hello," he greeted.

"Your Majesty," Trohm started, sounding distinctly uncomfortable.

"What's the matter?"

He didn't appear to be in danger or imprisoned, which were the only two options he could think that would ruffle his agent's otherwise unflappable demeanor.

The only other time he could imagine was when he heard Verity speaking to Trohm about how he had kept their liaison a secret from him.

But he had only been able to *hear* his agent during that conversation.

Knox felt his impatience growing when his agent still didn't answer.

"Trohm, tell me what is happening. That's an order from your king."

"Arfilmea has broken your engagement."

Out of everything his agent could have said, that possibility hadn't even crossed his mind.

Knox leaned forward. "Excuse me?" Why hadn't Aerue told him? Or Arfilmea, herself? For neither of them to have been up front about the decision meant there was more to it.

"I'm sorry, Your Majesty."

Was he? Of course, losing the political alliance wasn't ideal. But a ruler didn't necessarily need a partner to be effective. And his council certainly wouldn't be happy now that they wouldn't have a pure Eochronian heir.

On the bright side, he no longer had to juggle his duty to her and his desire for Verity, but there still had to be more or Trohm would look much more relaxed now that he had dropped the bombshell.

"There's more, isn't there?" he asked.

"Yes, Your Majesty."

"Well? Out with it, then."

"She's aligned herself with Eiz'm. They're engaged now."

The words came out in a rush and Knox had to run them over in his head a second time to make sure he had heard correctly.

It was one thing for her to break their engagement because she didn't want to be married, or even maybe acknowledging that she didn't want to be married to *him*, since it had become clear due to recent events that they did not feel romantically for each other on top of his sexual attraction for her dwindling.

But it was an entirely different matter for her to break their engagement and then stab him in the back by choosing his rival. He was an illegitimate ruler, and anyone with any respect for tradition would have thrown out his bid for the throne immediately. But with the backing of his former fiancée, offering a queen to Eiz'm's proposed king, his rival's coup suddenly had the best endorsement possible aside from Knox himself stepping down in support of him—which would never happen.

"When did this happen?" he asked.

"I'm not entirely sure, Your Majesty, but it's definitely a more recent development."

"She asked me to come back yesterday."

His agent frowned. "Then I suspect it was a ploy to entrap you. I believe it's been at least two human days since they made the decision. They only just announced it to the council though."

"How did they respond?"

"They seemed amenable to the turn of events."

Knox let out a slew of Eochronian curses that would have had his mother scolding him and his father mildly impressed.

"Any news about the Vruxols?"

His agent shook his head. "Not yet, Your Majesty. But no one on the ship seems to be talking about it which makes me wonder..."

It made him wonder, too. They were close enough that someone had to absolutely be aware of the threat, even aside from him warning individuals aboard the ship.

Perhaps Eiz'm was being ruthlessly smart in letting the danger become so imminent and pressing that he could easily sell his style of leadership to anyone still doubting him and holding loyalty to the crowned king.

Knox took a deep breath. "Okay, keep me apprised of the situation but be careful. I don't want you to put yourself in danger."

"It would be my responsibility to, Your Majesty, to serve you to the best of my ability."

"Our numbers are too limited for you to unnecessarily court danger. Promise me you'll do what you need to in order to stay safe. Without betraying your king, of course," he added. That last part should have been a given but given the way things were going, he couldn't take loyalty for granted anymore.

Knox closed the communication with Trohm and opened another one with Dr. Mak'en.

"How can I help you, Your Majesty?"

"I need a progress report on the human subjects, and I have another task for you."

"They've been improving in your absence but their active treatment was halted soon after you left, Your Majesty."

"On whose orders?" He already knew the answer, but he needed to know which side Dr. Mak'en had taken in the civil war that was brewing.

"Eiz'm's, Your Majesty."

At least she was being honest.

"And you followed them?"

"He intimidated the chefs, Your Majesty. The humans, my staff, and I have been left untouched for now, but I do not know what his plans are for us, or why he would put a stop to your initiative."

Knox didn't answer, though he was sure Eiz'm's reason was to push the idea that his campaign wouldn't have worked.

"You said they were doing well, Dr. Mak'en?"

"Yes, Your Majesty. Even with the cessation of their regular treatment, many of their percentages have continued to climb. Very promising results."

"How promising?"

"Well, none as impressive as the female or the one male," her voice dipped as she mentioned them, likely knowing he had more personal than professional feelings about the two best candidates, "but some have jumped up to another five percent since I last reported to you."

Not quite the progress he was hoping for but better than he expected given they were no longer consuming the genetic agents that were being slipped to them in their food three times a day.

"Can you find an alternative administration method that you can secretly continue without putting yourself or your team in danger?"

"Am I allowed to inject them, Your Majesty?"

Knox sighed. "Yes, Dr. Mak'en. You may. I leave their treatment in your capable hands. Keep me updated of the progress, and let me know if anyone bothers you. And I do mean *anyone.*"

"Yes, Your Majesty."

He closed the communication and stared at the ceiling before looking out the window of the master bedroom, to where he'd relocated.

The sky was a clear blue and he was desperate to go out and about to soak up more of the sun. Who knew how long he'd have the luxury now that *shit had hit the fan* as the humans said. Though, he couldn't understand why they would have that saying. It brought to mind a very vivid image he had a hard time believing had ever truly happened. If it ever had, though, it deserved to be memorialized in such an evocative phrase.

Decision made, he changed into normal human clothes and walked out to the backyard, forgoing his contraption, though he had left that set up by the window to continue storing star energy on the unfortunate chance that he was barred from using his own royal suite once he got back home.

He felt the sun on his face and soaking into his skin, and closed his eyes, allowing himself to physically relax as much as possible.

His problems were by no means over but they were far away and he didn't have to deal with them right in that moment. They would still be there after a long session of sunbathing.

23

VERITY

BY THE TIME her father returned, it was night out. Had been for a while. Which meant he'd been avoiding her for over thirteen hours.

Yes, she was sure a large amount of that time was spent doing important duties she could only imagine, but he had to eat some time. And he hadn't checked in with her via text during lunch or even dinner time.

She had no disillusions that he hadn't checked in with Ben or McDonald, though she suspected that he might have also been giving poor McDonald the silent treatment.

For his part, her second guard had been more attentive and on her ass every time she moved from one room to another. He was more annoying than Peter Pan's shadow, following her around everywhere, but other than kicking him out of her room before her therapy session, she didn't give him a hard time about guarding her.

Bored from doing nothing while waiting for her father to return, Verity decided she would take a bath and hopefully soak some of the stress out of her muscles. She loved showers because of how fast they went but sometimes, she just wanted a hot bath.

"I'm taking a bath," she called out to her guards on the first floor. "And if anyone comes into my bathroom without knocking first, I'll kill you."

"Yes, ma'am," McDonald and Ben's voices replied in unison.

They were patronizing her, but she didn't care. As long as they didn't barge in on her, that's all that mattered for the time being.

She grabbed her towel and went into the bathroom, and started running the faucet. She grabbed the epsom salt from underneath her sink and poured it into the hot water.

While she waited for the level to rise high enough for her to enter, she checked her social media on her phone.

More and more posts about the mystery healer on the Vegas Strip were filling her timelines and she was curious if anyone actually had anything useful to share. But they were all filled with stupid guesses and more than a few thirsty people saying they'd like the handsome stranger to heal them any time.

She rolled her eyes. They had no idea what they were asking for. And while she had faith in the hospital's finding that the girl truly had been healed of cancer, there was no guarantee that Knox hadn't sneakily done something else to alter her, like he'd clearly done to her and the other human captives on his ship. Trohm had even confirmed it, though not with enough specifics for her to figure out how it was happening and to even *guess* what was really happening inside her body.

By the time she looked up again, her bath was ready. She turned off the water, stripped off her clothes, and climbed into the tub, closing her eyes as she leaned back against the porcelain edge.

She just had to be sure to not fall asleep. She wasn't keen on having another near-death by drowning experience. One was more than enough to last what was hopefully going to be a long, normal lifetime.

. . .

VERITY WOKE to pounding on the door.

"Are you okay in there?" Ben's voice came through the wood.

"Yeah," she called. "Why?"

"You've been in there for an hour and your father just came home."

She sat up and pulled the plug. "I'll be right there."

Ben didn't answer but she could hear his footsteps descending the staircase. Probably didn't want to be caught near the bathroom where the General's daughter was naked on the other side of the door.

She wrapped the towel around her and ran across the hall into her bedroom where she dressed as fast as she ever had, faster even than the quick changes she'd had to do during the freshman performance showcase when she'd been in three different pieces with very different costumes.

Verity ran down the stairs and found her father in the kitchen, grabbing a bite to eat.

Honestly, she had expected him to have eaten in his office. Maybe he really *was* busy all day.

He nodded at her in greeting.

She returned the gesture, not wanting to be the first to speak in case it set him off into another argument. Her father, like her, could put a pin in something and then resume hours later as if it truly were putting a pause on the conversation, without any time spent cooling down.

Realistically speaking, she probably learned that behavior from him.

She just hoped this wasn't one of those cases. She hated dancing around him like she was afraid of setting off a time bomb, but that's exactly what she was doing.

Verity walked around him to go get something from the fridge herself. She wasn't particularly hungry, and anything that she did consume would probably make a reappearance sooner than later anyway, but she needed something to do.

She she pulled out a can of ginger ale and put some ice cubes into a glass from the cabinet. She poured herself two fingers of the golden soda before putting the can back into the refrigerator.

Maybe it would just settle her stomach in general as a precaution.

She had eaten a little during dinner time but not much since she wasn't too hungry then, either, but she hadn't thrown up from that yet, which she took as a tentatively good sign that she didn't have faith would last very long.

She propped herself against the sink and took a sip, scanning the room, not letting her eyes linger on her father too long lest he ask her what's on her mind.

Right now, it was how to continue their conversation productively—or, more accurately—wanting to but having no idea of how to actually do it. Somewhere in the back was also thoughts on whether Knox would be coming for her soon or if he was just amusing himself by making his presence known and keeping her on edge.

Part of her wanted to believe he was sadistically toying with her but that didn't sit well with what she knew of him. He didn't seem like someone who enjoyed the pain of others. She could be wrong in her assessment of him, though. For all she knew, it was only what he'd *shown* her. It could have been an act, or a partial truth, but she liked to have thought her assessment of people was correct. Though, maybe she shouldn't have faith in her abilities any more given what happened with Tristan really being Trohm.

Everything related to the frustrating alien king sent her on a useless, circular train of thought.

Her father finally finished eating and rose to put his stuff in the sink, requiring her to scoot over.

"You have something to discuss?" he asked, keeping his attention on his hands scrubbing the the plate long after all the food residue was already gone.

"Do you?" she asked, throwing it back at him.

She knew full well that her father could wolf down food when he wanted to. He could have finished his meal in no more than ten bites and disappeared into his study or his room upstairs if he truly wanted to avoid her. His sticking around so long meant that he was wanting to talk to her like she did him.

He grabbed a glass and poured himself some water from the filtered tap.

"I decided you're right."

Verity pushed herself upright until she was standing. "You did?" Dare she ask about what? Or would that be rubbing it in too much?

"You deserve answers, and while I can't give you all of them—because there are things even I don't know," he explained before she could cut in, "I shouldn't be keeping the information I do have to myself, especially since it has to do with your health."

He walked into his office where McDonald had been manning the security cameras. She followed, passing McDonald on his way out.

Her father sat on one side of the couch, leaving enough space for her to sit next to him.

She did, gingerly.

She'd never been physically afraid of her father, and she wasn't now, but she was scared of being in a situation she'd never been in before.

An overly cautious approach she had adopted too thoroughly since her return. She would always get nervous before an audition or performance but this was a next-level form of anxiety that wasn't tied to specific scenarios, and was therefore unavoidable.

"What did you want to tell me?"

"I know why you were kidnapped by them."

If Verity hadn't already been sitting, she would've collapsed onto the couch at that very unexpected pronouncement. Did that also mean he had *expected* it to happen? And if so, did that mean he wasn't actually trying to stop it? That didn't make sense. Her father had *definitely* been fighting to protect her when they had invaded their home, and his unconscious and bleeding body hadn't been an act on his part.

But it seemed like even if he hadn't expected it to happen with certainty, whatever her father knew about her and why the aliens would want to abduct her made it a possibility he must have considered.

Her father continued without waiting for her to ask a clarifying question. Maybe he needed to get it all out for fear he'd stop halfway through, or maybe he didn't realize that her mind was spinning so much with the one pronouncement that he figured she was just waiting for him to keep going.

"When I was first offered this job, at this base, ASE had recently just found a meteorite."

She already knew this part. It was a space collection mission the greater public knew nothing about, and she only knew the basics of. But she had no idea how that had anything to do with her situation.

"They discovered alien DNA on it and started testing it."

He was staring at her in a way that made it clear he was hoping she'd fill in the gaps herself but she was at a loss.

"Once it was determined it was safe for humans, they started experimenting with fusing it to humans. The STFs are the first group to ever have the DNA grafted into their genomes."

She had so many questions. She didn't know where to start. "All of them?" she managed to choke out.

"No, only the best were given the option to participate in this experimental program."

"Who?"

"Verity—"

"Who, Dad?"

He named a few, many of whom she'd never kept track of because they were older and had left the base to integrate into normal Air Force bases while she was still a child. But in the list were two she easily recognized. *Harrison* and *Tenner*.

"Ben!" she shouted.

"Yes?" he called back. From somewhere upstairs.

"Get in here!"

She heard him approach and stared at the doorway in anticipation of his appearance.

He quickly took in the scene of her sitting next to her father and stepped closer until he was fully in the room.

"Sir?" he asked.

Was he worried she'd told her father about their kiss? Or was he worried she finally found out about how he was genetically engineered as part of some crazy experiment?

"I've told my daughter about the program. Perhaps you would like to explain your choice to participate?"

They shared a look with each other, and Verity knew for a fact that she was still missing pieces of the puzzle.

Ben took a seat in the armchair near her and leaned forward on his knees as he spoke, "When the General picked me, I felt honored. And I was told it would help me better serve our country, so of course I agreed to—"

"Be the government's lab rat?" she finished for him.

Ben shook his head. "It wasn't like that."

She turned back to her father. "That still doesn't explain what that has to do with me. I'm not one of your airmen."

Her father cleared his throat. "Before we moved, I was in talks with this base and ASE for a long time. Your mom was pregnant with you and—"

She raised her hand to stop him and ran to the upstairs bathroom as she gave into the sudden urge to throw up. As she ran up the steps, she almost tripped twice but luckily, she was able to reach the toilet before she made a mess in the hall but she felt like she was expelling all her internal organs with the amount of retching she did.

Though she was throwing up her food, her nausea was more to do with finally putting together what her father was trying to tell her than the food that had otherwise been sitting happily in her stomach.

If this conversation hadn't happened, there was a chance—probably a slim one, but still a chance—that she could have skipped this unfortunate habit today for the first time since the whole mess started.

She finally finished and flushed. Before she turned on the faucet, she listened to see if her father and Ben were talking in her absence.

All she could hear was silence between them.

She quickly brushed her teeth and made her way back downstairs to them.

"So," she said, standing in the doorway, unable to be closer to them without wanting to smack both of them. "I'm also an experiment?"

Her father couldn't meet her gaze.

"But instead of having the choice to *volunteer* to have scientists play mix and match with my genes, you made the decision without me before I was even me?" she demanded. "Did mom even know?"

He shook his head. "No. She had no idea."

"Does Dr. Lane know?"

Her father nodded. "Yes. She's been aware of your special circumstances the whole time."

"I'm a test tube baby."

"Well, that's not strictly—"

She glared at her father, effectively cutting him off from whatever weak defense he was about to mount on the basis of a linguistic technicality.

She turned on her heel and walked out of the room.

"I need some time alone," she said to the guys, not bothering to warn them off from following her. "McDonald!"

"Yes?" he called from the back room of the first floor.

"I'm going upstairs."

"On your six," he said, and she heard him follow her up to the second floor.

She waited for him to reach the landing before she pulled him into her room and shut the door.

He stared at her like she was crazy. "What are you doing? Your dad will kill me for being in here alone with you!"

"He won't touch you," she assured him. "Besides, he's going to stay at least ten feet away from me if he knows what's good for him."

McDonald looked uncomfortable at getting in between the daughter-father dispute but he wisely didn't ask for any more details of her cryptic announcement. And if he left her alone, he'd be shirking his guard duties so he couldn't exactly abandon her either.

She'd definitely have to set him up with a dancer to compensate him for his time. But for now, she grabbed her laptop off her desk and lay down on her bed with her headphones, and pulled up one of her favorite TV shows on a streaming website. She settled into her pillows and prepared for some mindless entertainment to distract her from the horrifying and disturbing knowledge that her father was ultimately responsible for her traumatic kidnapping.

She needed to process it, and she couldn't exactly ask for Dr. Hudson's help this time. She'd have to do it on her own, and it would take time, but she wasn't going to do it tonight.

VERITY WAS in the middle of watching yet another fight demonstration by the instructor when she saw Ben touch his earwig, clearly listening to a message being relayed.

His gaze met hers, but he didn't give any indication of what news he had just received other than to whisper something to

McDonald before walking away from the asphalt and back towards the houses.

She looked to McDonald who shook his head, and she turned back to the instructor who was staring at her judgmentally.

She glared back until the instructor looked away and resumed their explanation of the new technique for the day.

Fight class continued without any interruptions or mishaps of her accidentally injuring anyone, qualifying it as a small success in her mind. But Ben hadn't returned from whatever errand he ran off to do, and she was starting to wonder where he'd gone. Maybe he was trying to track down Trohm?

But when she and McDonald arrived back at her home, she realized it was much worse.

Her father met her at the door, a solemn expression on his face.

"What happened?" she asked, a sinking feeling already settling in her gut.

"Ben is dead."

The news was like a punch to the gut, and she fought the urge to crumple over in despair.

He had died while she was still mad at him. She couldn't say goodbye. She couldn't tell him that she still loved him—even if not the way she had once thought she did.

And now someone had ripped that away from him, and her.

No, not *someone*. She knew exactly who had done this, and there was going to be hell to pay.

"How?" she finally gasped.

"Beheaded," her father answered grimly.

Her nightmares had come true. Literally.

She'd never believed in people who claimed to see or hear the future but the dream gave her shivers.

"Is—is he in there?" she asked. Was his corpse lying in the living room? Her room like an even more morbid version of the famous mob movie scene with the horse head?

He shook his head.

She entered the home, looking around as if she could maybe tell where he had last been before his life had been unjustly cut short. But her house looked the same as it had when she left that morning.

On a strange instinct, she ran upstairs and into her bedroom.

Lying on her pillow was another note.

She grabbed it and smiled.

Instead of another promise from him, it was an address.

24

KNOX

KNOX WAS DREAMING when he awakened by sirens going off at the air base.

He hadn't slept the whole time he had been on Earth until he suddenly felt the urge to now that he was alone in Zeph's home, and nothing to entertain him. Going back to the Vegas Strip alone wasn't as interesting as when he had a companion and now that all the humans there were likely searching for him, it wasn't the best place for him to be spending more time.

At least in this small community, he had relative anonymity.

But something was clearly happening with the humans, and he was tempted to go investigate himself but he was sure that their high alert included having their entire arsenal ready with a hair-trigger, so he would wait until things calmed down again.

Then he heard the knocking on his door.

Anyone who he might expect to visit him could enter without doing so, so he made his way and pulled up the Eochronian security monitor to see who was on the other side.

Once he saw who it was, he immediately opened the door.

A beautiful and very pissed-off Verity stood before him, her hand raised to knock again.

That same hand moved with Eochronian speed that he couldn't tell her intention until it was too late.

She had slapped him.

Prepared this time, he caught her other hand as it attempted to make contact with the other side of his face.

He didn't want a matching set of handprints on his cheeks.

He grabbed both wrists and pulled her inside, then rotated them so he could kick the door closed.

He didn't need any of Zeph's human neighbors to realize there was someone else staying in the house.

They stood in the dark living room, close enough for their breath to intermingle.

Verity was breathing heavily and he couldn't help but appreciate how her chest was enticingly rising and falling.

He took another step closer, pressing them tightly together.

He brought his face down to hers, their lips almost touching. "Why are you here, Verity?"

"You know why," she hissed.

"Do I?"

"Ben is dead."

"Really?" How interesting. "And you think I killed him?"

She tried to shake out of his grasp, but she wasn't strong enough to. "Of course you did! You've hated him since the moment you met him."

Not *quite* true but close enough. He hadn't had any feelings about him when he was first brought on board until he had learned of his close bond with Verity thanks to the ugly emotion of jealousy.

"And my not liking the man is somehow proof that I'm his murderer? Doesn't your country follow the belief that the accused are '*innocent* until proven guilty'?"

"It doesn't apply to you."

"Why not?"

"Because you're not human."

"Should your morality really be dependent on the other party? Doesn't that make your moral compass subjective and therefore not infallible? What if I were a dog?"

"Don't insult that amazing species by comparing yourself to humanity's best friend."

He raised an eyebrow. "Not 'man's best friend'?"

"I updated it." She sighed. "And unfortunately, dogs accused of hurting people are assumed guilty. They deserve better since most dogs only act badly if they're provoked or untrained."

"Which category do I fall under for this supposed crime of mine?"

"There's nothing *supposed* about it. It's a crime to murder someone."

"Agreed," he said. "But my use of the word refers to the crime being mine. Which it is not."

"I don't believe you."

"That's a shame, but it doesn't change the truth."

"If only," she muttered.

She sounded so sad in that small utterance released her arms and instead pulled her into an embrace, his need to comfort her overriding everything else.

Surprisingly, she didn't fight him off, but let herself be held for a few moments before she pushed lightly on his chest.

He let her go and they stood staring at each other.

It felt like forever since he'd last seen her, and now that she was here, he almost didn't know what to do. Almost.

He put on his armor and grabbed her, taking her out to the backyard since he didn't want to destroy the building, and called his ship.

It arrived, but as it was reassembling itself, he heard the sounds of guns being cocked and likely aimed at him.

She had set a trap for him, and he'd fallen into it without any resistance because he'd been so overcome with her surprise visit and intoxicating presence.

Aerue had been right. She was a dangerous distraction.

Had he not been so preoccupied, he would have heard the guards coming much sooner and would have brought the ship into the house—walls of the house be damned—and left with her without having to venture outside. They wouldn't have been able to shoot him down, and he'd have accomplished his final goal on Earth, allowing him to return home to deal with the issues there.

Now, he was stuck, because even though he could probably survive long enough to take out many of the soldiers sniping for him, there was a chance at least one would kill him. And if it didn't, the shower of bullets would almost assuredly kill Verity. So, he let them approach and restrain him with titanium shackles and didn't fight as they marched him toward the base. Before any of the humans could touch his ship, he disassembled it again with a tap of his fingers on his other wrist while the guards on his sides weren't looking.

They surprisingly didn't have one walking behind him, and Verity was walking in front of him.

If she was nervous by having him watching her, she didn't show it. Her stride was fast and stable with each step. Confidence radiated from her. She had gotten over her fears about her transformation. Or, she was effectively pushing it down in the face of danger.

Regardless of her current and misplaced certainty that he'd been subdued, he was sure that her backup had interrupted her as much as him. She'd likely be coming to visit him again to finish ripping into him for his perceived crimes.

He looked forward to it. Because once he got her alone, she'd finally be his and he could defend his throne and prove to his people—once and for all—that he was their rightful king. For now, he'd have to bide his time.

ALIEN PRONUNCIATION GUIDE

Verity - Ver-i-tee

Eochron - ee-yo-kron
Eochronian - ee-yo-crone-ian

Aerue - aye-rue
Arfilmea - ar-fil-me-ah
Eiz'm - eyes-um
Knox - nox
Trohm - tro-m
Quallokh - kwal-lock
Zrelhlm - zrell-lem

AUTHOR'S NOTE

Important note: authors live on reviews. And so, I ask you, my wonderful reader, to leave a review on your favorite retailer, and recommend this book to your friends.

If you would like a free book and to be kept in the loop about all my future publishing endeavors, subscribe to my newsletter at www.zarahoffman.com/subscribe

ACKNOWLEDGMENTS

As always, thank you so much to my readers. I couldn't do this without you.

I also want to give a special shoutout to my *viewers*. This was the first story I talked about on my YouTube channel and the excitement I got from my subscribers really helped me stay motivated as I worked on it in the crazy quarantine and lockdown periods of 2020.

I'd like to thank my cover designer, Alivia Anders of White Rabbit Book Design for the gorgeous cover. I cannot tell you how many people have complimented it.

Thank you to all my early readers who helped make this story the best it could be: Charlie, Dania, Hannah, Maria, Natalie, and Regina.

I want to send a special thanks to Natalie, again, for your military experience and willingness for me to run ideas by you in a running text message conversation.

ABOUT THE AUTHOR

Zara Hoffman is a graduate student in the NYU Masters in Publishing Program and has been writing since she was eight years old. She spends most of her time doing homework and writing new stories because if she didn't, her head would likely explode. Her books are for young adults or the young at heart. After all, growing up is overrated.

www.zarahoffman.com
zarahoffman@zarahoffman.com

ALSO BY ZARA HOFFMAN

The Belgrave Legacy

The Belgrave Legacy

Unmoored

Taming the Alpha

Stellar Blood

Obscure Origin

Sacred Souls

www.ingramcontent.com/pod-product-compliance
Lightning Source LLC
Chambersburg PA
CBHW032119170626
46808CB00006B/2013

* 9 7 8 0 9 9 9 1 9 8 6 4 3 *